GREATEST ENEMY

AN AMERICAN MERCENARY THRILLER

JASON KASPER

SEVERN RIVER
PUBLISHING

Severn River Publishing
SevernRiverBooks.com

ISBN: 978-1-64875-484-5 (Paperback)

ALSO BY JASON KASPER

American Mercenary Series
Greatest Enemy
Offer of Revenge
Dark Redemption
Vengeance Calling
The Suicide Cartel
Terminal Objective

Shadow Strike Series
The Enemies of My Country
Last Target Standing
Covert Kill
Narco Assassins
Beast Three Six

Spider Heist Thrillers
The Spider Heist
The Sky Thieves
The Manhattan Job
The Fifth Bandit

Standalone Thriller
Her Dark Silence

To find out more about Jason Kasper and his books, visit
severnriverbooks.com/authors/jason-kasper

To Bravo One—

I understand.

See you at the final TIC.

HATE

Res firma mitescere nescit

-A firm resolve does not know how to weaken

1

June 1, 2008
Park Ridge, Illinois

The house was silent, and I passed through its shadows like a ghost.

Moonlight filtered through the horizontal slats of the blinds, its dull glow mottled by the trees and casting hazy shadows over me. As I rounded the corner of the entryway, the only sound that could be heard above the rustle of my clothes and the whisper of my footsteps on the carpet was the low hum of a refrigerator, its surface reflecting the twin green clocks of a microwave and oven.

I pivoted around a corner, both hands maneuvering the .22 pistol that hovered just beneath my field of vision. A crimson light marked the corner of an idling flat screen on the wall, and beneath it the black, gaping maw of a fireplace. Moving past them, I stopped at the corner to see a hallway receding into blackness.

After releasing one gloved hand from the gun, I made a fist and rapped three times on the wall.

White light abruptly framed a door at the end of the hall, and the rack of a shotgun slide echoed throughout the house. In an instant, the door swung open and flooded the hallway with glaring light. I stepped back into the shadows as the long barrel of a 12-gauge Mossberg appeared from the door frame.

As the man holding the shotgun emerged from the room and swung the barrel toward me, I shot him twice in the gut.

He stumbled backward as the quick barks of my .22 faded, his back striking the far wall as he slumped into a seated position. One hand clutched his stomach while the other maintained a tenuous grip on the shotgun.

I stepped into the light and said, "Hello, Peter. I'm David Rivers."

He squinted up at me, panting in disbelief as a glimmer of recognition crossed his eyes.

"How's Laila?" he asked.

"This is between us now. You started our first conversation, and now I'm starting our last."

He swung the shotgun barrel toward my face and pulled the trigger.

A hollow click sounded.

"That's odd," I said, sliding my pistol into my belt. I walked forward and took the shotgun from his hand, which slid down his lap and fell limply to the floor. Then I reached into my pocket for the shells and began slipping them into the loading port.

He assumed a fearful, obedient look of submission, his now-empty hand uniting with the other over his stomach as bright red blood streamed through his fingers.

"Don't," he whispered between ragged breaths. "I can pay you... call them... get the ambulance."

"The last time we spoke, you lectured me on revenge. Do you want to lecture me now?"

"I never saw you, man. Just go. Please."

I loaded the final shell and shook my head.

"I told you this would happen, Peter. And I know you've probably talked shit without consequence on a thousand other occasions. But you finally did it at the wrong time to the wrong fucking person. And now"—I racked the slide to load a shell into the chamber—"you're about to get smoked in the face with your own shotgun."

Balling his hands into nervous fists against his bleeding gut, he cringed as if expecting me to slap him. "Listen to me for one fucking second. Just hear me out—"

"I gave you the chance to kill yourself, but you didn't have the brains or the balls to do the honorable thing. Maybe your dad didn't teach you right, or maybe you were born a coward and it's in your blood. Either way, I'm giving you a chance to face the consequences of your actions like you've never had to do."

"I've got close to twenty grand in the bedroom safe; just take it and go. The code is 62-29-99."

My face slid into a grin. "Peter, you're not listening. Accept your fate. You asked for me, and now you've got me. And no one's going to avenge you, because I'm swallowing a gun in a few hours. This is how your life is going to end."

"I'm begging you, I shouldn't have treated Laila like that. I didn't mean to... I'm sorry, I'm so fucking sorry—"

"Try and have some dignity at your death. You only get one."

"I'll do anything, just please don't fucking do this."

I angled the shotgun barrel level with his face. "At least you didn't cry."

At this, he began weeping like Laila had on the night he called her.

"Goodbye, Peter," I said, firing the Mossberg with a deafening blast.

His head vanished in an explosion of blood and smoke. As his shoulders slumped to the side, I lowered the barrel and watched the eerie postmortem twitch of his shoulders.

Then I dropped the shotgun at my feet, turned, and walked out of the house.

* * *

The neon liquor store sign glowed in the darkness, its seedy glare the same in every state I'd ever visited. I accelerated toward it, the tires of my twelve-year-old Explorer rumbling over the uneven surface of the pavement, which was saturated with rain that had only stopped minutes ago. The rest of the storefronts along the empty street were dark, now visible only by the distant radiance of streetlights until my headlights swept over them as I passed.

I sped up as I neared the liquor store. It was moments away from closing for the night, which I had realized abruptly when I reached my hotel and found that the bottle I'd packed was nearly empty.

After pulling into the abandoned lot, I found a dark parking spot between streetlights and then killed the engine. Snatching my backpack from the passenger seat, I hastily unzipped the main compartment to reveal my laptop case, which bore the scars of half a decade of travel. I paused for a moment before reaching past the laptop, feeling around in the bag until my fingers touched a cool, textured grip.

I withdrew the Ruger revolver, a steel bulldog that weighed more than double the pistol I'd just used to wound Peter. Opening the cylinder, I checked that it was fully loaded with six rounds stamped .454 CASULL, each capable of killing any big game on the planet. Satisfied, I snapped the cylinder shut and carefully slid the Ruger into my waistband before pulling my shirttail over it.

I set the backpack on the passenger seat, then stepped into the warm, humid air and strode toward the entrance.

An elderly vagrant in a green military jacket limped toward me from the side of the store.

"Hey, son," he called, "you got any change? Hey, son!"

I walked past him and pushed open the door, stepping into the bright lights of the store's interior.

A male voice called to me from behind the register, "We close in five minutes."

Walking through the aisles, I scanned the shelves until I found the rows of glass bottles with reassuringly familiar labels. I passed the scotches and whiskeys, then came to a halt in front of the house selection of bourbon. My eyes drifted to the top shelf, and I sighed in relief as I stretched out my hand to grasp the neck of a single, large bottle.

I brought it to chest height and cradled the bottom with my other hand as I appraised the neatly printed letters spelling WOODFORD RESERVE.

I frowned when I saw that the otherwise flawless bottle was marred with a cheap, lopsided green sticker that said, CLOSING TIME WINE & SPIRITS: $62.99.

As I approached the register, the college-aged Indian man behind the counter watched me.

"You look like a man on a mission."

I set down the bottle in front of him. "Yeah. Didn't realize I was running out of bourbon until just now."

"Busy night?"

"Something like that."

"You need a mixer?"

"And consume all those empty calories? I'm trying to live forever."

He examined the sticker on the bottle and typed the price into his register. "$68.16," he said.

I looked up at the vertical American flag suspended from the ceiling behind him, the drooping ripples in its fabric accumulating wide semicircles of dust.

"$68.16," he repeated, sliding the bottle into a brown paper bag and setting it upright on the counter.

I counted out four bills from my wallet and handed them to him. "Keep the change."

"Thanks. Need your receipt?"

"No."

"Have a good one."

I compressed the bag around the neck of the bottle and said, "I most certainly will. You do the same."

When I stepped outside into the damp night air, a voice beside me yelled, "Hey!"

The old man who had asked me for change was still standing there, and his weathered, unshaven face fixed on mine even as his shoulders swayed with drunkenness.

"Don't you ignore me," he demanded, his eyes welling up with tears. "I'm a veteran, goddammit."

I stopped and faced him, glancing down at the faded patches on his jacket. "Where'd you serve at, Staff Sergeant?"

"I was in Dak To in '67, fighting for your country. That's Vietnam, son."

I tucked the bottle under one arm and reached for my wallet. I pulled out a stack of bills, folded them in half, and handed them to him.

"That's everything I've got, Sarge. Treat yourself to the good stuff."

Returning to my truck, I settled into the driver's seat and slammed the door shut behind me. I opened the backpack and was sliding the bottle of bourbon alongside my laptop when I heard the sudden, piercing wail of police sirens.

I looked out the windshield at the empty parking lot and, beyond it, the orbiting flashes of red and blue lights reflecting off storefronts in the distance. I took a deep breath and released it, then reached under my shirt to pull out the Ruger.

Rotating the revolver upward between my chest and the steering wheel, I pressed the warm steel ring of the muzzle against the underside of my jaw. My right finger settled on the smooth curve of the trigger, and I whispered to myself:

"Three."

The headlights of the first police car pierced the night, and were followed immediately by a second one.

"Two."

I became lost in the sirens' howling wails as their volume increased to a roar.

"One."

The glare of the flashing lights grew in intensity, nearly blinding me as I squinted into the flickering red-and-blue nothingness.

"See ya."

My finger tensed on the trigger as the police cars roared past my vehicle, their sirens receding as they sped along the wet street.

I released what seemed like an endless exhale, then lowered the pistol to my lap and took a few measured breaths. I slipped the Ruger back into my waistband and pulled my shirt over it once more.

Starting my truck, I turned on the headlights and pulled forward, gliding the car through a long puddle before turning onto the street and driving away from the sound of police sirens that, by then, had faded almost entirely.

* * *

As I walked down the hotel hallway toward my room with the heavy backpack slung over my left shoulder, I felt an overwhelming rush of relief. I would be able to spend my final hours drinking and writing, the last two exquisite pleasures in my life.

Coming to a stop before room 629, I fished the key card out of my pocket and slid it into the slot above the handle. When the light flashed green, I pushed open the door and stepped inside the modest room.

As I let the door slam shut behind me, my eyes fell to the corner table backed by a rolling chair. There, I would compose my final passage, my magnum opus. It would crown a thousand fragmented pieces of writing that had accumulated on the laptop like cancer cells over the nights spent sitting alone in the darkness, looking deep inside myself and becoming increasingly sickened by what I found.

My eyes ticked downward, registering wet footprints on the patterned carpet. In that same instant, I heard a man's voice coming from my left.

"Get your hands up, shithead."

My stomach dropped.

I held my hands open at waist level and looked through the bathroom doorway to the end of an automatic pistol emerging from the shadows, its barrel extending into a suppressor that was aimed at my chest.

A second voice said, "All the way up, David. Do it, or you're dead."

I glanced up to see the end of another handgun suppressor leveled at my face, the man holding it tucked behind the edge of the wall in front of the bed.

My mind raced in disbelief. I took a final breath, and did the only thing I could.

Yanking on my shirtfront with one hand, I seized the rubber grips of the Ruger with the other. I'd drawn the pistol in a split second, and was just beginning to rotate the barrel upward when the first man tackled me into the wall with the force of a freight train.

The revolver tumbled from my grasp as his shoulders drove me to the floor. Before I could recover from the initial impact, the second man advanced on me and delivered a crushing overhead blow to the side of my face.

My vision blurred, my mouth filled with thick blood, and pain exploded in my skull. The first man rolled me onto my back, yanking my upper body off the ground by my collar. In a blindingly fast three-part motion, he bounced my head off the ground, against the wall, and off the ground again.

I involuntarily coughed up an explosion of blood before he rolled me back onto my stomach. One of the men stripped the backpack from my left arm while the other jerked my hands upward to the small of my back.

I winced and grunted, "mother*fucker*," into the carpet as my wrists were cinched together with a narrow plastic restraint. The man straddling my back roughly frisked me, removing the contents of my pockets. I heard the rustling of paper and sloshing of bourbon as the other man searched my bag.

With half of my face smashed into the floor and my voice slurred with the blood in my mouth, I said, "You know, for a second there I thought you were the police."

The man above me grasped the side of my neck, applying his body weight to pin me down further into the carpet. The boots belonging to the second man stepped in front of my face, and as I tried to roll my eyes upward, the end of a pistol suppressor was pressed against my temple, forcing my head back to the floor.

One of the men responded with a curt voice spoken between angry breaths.

"It would be better for you if we were. Trust me on that. And we know you killed Peter McAlister."

"What makes you say that?"

"Because we watched you do it."

"No, you didn't."

"We watched you get the spare key from the brick in the front walkway. Then we stood over him at the end of the hallway before his brains had dried on the wall. Is that specific enough for you, David?"

"We're getting there."

"This is where you tell us who paid you to kill him."

"No, it isn't."

At this, the hand on the side of my neck rotated around my jugular and squeezed, cutting off my air. The man pulled me up by my throat, lifting my chest off the ground before spinning me sideways. My shoulders slammed against the wall as I came to rest in a slouched sitting position.

When I opened my mouth to hollowly gasp for air, he slid the pistol suppressor between my teeth, pushing it to the back of my throat before releasing the pressure on my jugular. I snorted desperate breaths through my nostrils as I caught my first full glimpse of my attacker. His chest was as wide as my shoulders, and his dark eyes blazed with fury behind the handgun. I tried to pull my face away from the pistol, but he grabbed the back of my head and forced the suppressor deeper into my mouth.

"Talk around the gun. Who paid you to kill him?"

"How am I supposed to spit in your face with a pistol in my mouth?" I mumbled.

I heard the chirp of a radio, followed by a tinny voice that said, *"Black, Red."*

Somewhere to my right, the second man responded, "Go for Black."

"You're going to love what I found in his truck. This guy is coming with us."

My mind raced through the contents of my vehicle, settling on the black ballistic nylon bag hidden under a tarp.

The man hovering over me leaned in and said, "This isn't finished," before pulling the pistol out of my mouth, raising it high to the side, and swinging it back down across my head. I flinched a split second before the metal cracked against my skull.

Then, my entire world went black.

REVELATION

Omnes vulnerant, ultima necat

-All wound, the last kills

2

The raging sun slipped under the horizon, the endless sky blushing to a blazing orange hue in the final minutes before darkness.

The sight could not have been more welcomed by the men who watched it.

From the first moment it became visible until it descended into the other side of the earth, the sun over Saudi Arabia turned the world around us into an oven. Its merciless rays were amplified by the featureless, hard-packed sand that extended flat as a pool table in all directions and out to the horizon.

By the time nightfall arrived, my company of Army Rangers had already been sitting in rows on the ground beside the dirt airstrip for hours, sweating in desert camouflage chemical suits. Our gas mask carriers were slung between our thighs, and on top of those folded kit bags contained vests loaded with ammunition, grenades, and canteens that were pinned across our waists by harness straps from our static line parachutes. Massive rucksacks were attached to our hips below shoebox-sized reserves, adding an additional hundred-pound anchor to our load.

The majority of us were nineteen-year-old privates, and our purpose at any given time was dictated by slightly older team and squad leaders. Although we were young, if the government wanted to parachute 154 Americans behind enemy lines to capture an airfield and begin ransacking their way across enemy territory until the commanding general said to stop, then Rangers were the force of choice.

Until I had proven myself in Afghanistan the previous summer, my daily routine consisted of being punched in the stomach, thrown into wall lockers in the squad area, kicked in the ribs as I did push-ups on command, and conducting the aptly named "electric chair," which involved squatting against the wall while holding a twenty-pound machine gun tripod with arms extended—within minutes the body began to shake uncontrollably, giving the appearance of being electrocuted.

That type of personal and professional development was completely independent of structured training that included road marches, shooting, practicing raids, and patrolling through the woods late into the night and oftentimes into the following day.

The collective result of those efforts culminated in the scene before me: a group of men completely desensitized to violence, charged with testosterone, and bored by weeks of living in tents on the remote Saudi airfield. We had spent the days of March 2003 waiting for the Iraq invasion, and now required only the arrival of our airplanes to enter our second war in as many years.

Remington was seated on the ground beside me, his lanky features and darting eyes beginning to vanish in the fading light.

Speaking in a barely intelligible strain of Alabamian, he said, "You better give them hell up at West Point, David. Represent Gun Six. Who's supposed to be on my gun team once you're gone?"

"We've got to make it through the invasion first, Remy. And I'm not reporting to West Point until June."

"How many times you applied to that place, anyway?"

"Just twice."

"Who ever thought of you a-going to college," he drawled. He paused to spit a stream of wintergreen tobacco juice onto the dirt. "What did Sarah say when she found out you got in?"

"It'll delay the wedding a bit. She wasn't thrilled."

"Four years ain't a bit, Slick."

"Five. I have a year of prep school first."

"You think she's gonna wait around for that? Lemme see that picture again."

He often made the same request, though he had met her in person numerous times. I reached into a shoulder pocket and pulled out the dog-eared photograph I had been carrying with me since Afghanistan.

I handed it to him. "We've been together since we were fifteen, and I look like a fucking male model. She'll wait."

He turned on the red lens headlamp that hung around his neck, and its glow illuminated the glossy image of a slim, brunette teenager who was holding a teddy bear and smiling coyly at the camera from her college dorm room.

Remington examined it closely. "I hope I find me a girl like that someday."

"You're the best motherfucker I've ever met." I switched my tone to imitate a deep Southern accent. "You'll find her, Remy."

Handing the picture back, he said, "I don't talk like that."

He talked exactly like that. Even when objecting, he pronounced "that" with two syllables: *thay-att*.

The First Sergeant shouted, "PLANES!"

Remington killed his headlamp, and I stuffed the picture back in my shoulder pocket as the churning hum of turboprops grew in volume. An MC-130 Combat Talon appeared out of the darkness and touched down on the airstrip several hundred meters away, roaring past us as three identical transport planes landed in rapid succession. They slowed to a halt and began turning around, whipping stinging sand across our faces. Remington and I struggled to rise as airfield staff moved from man to man, helping us to our feet.

The walk toward the aircraft quickly became a feat of extreme endurance. The two hundred meters that stretched between us and the planes felt like as many miles. Burdened by the weight of that much gear strapped to that many inconvenient places, our every movement was accomplished only through very small, duck-waddle steps that left us in excruciating pain. Airfield staff came to our rescue, lifting up the weight of our rucks while we staggered forward and helping to shuttle exhausted Rangers to the birds for boarding.

My line of jumpers reached the third aircraft and shuffled onto a ramp beneath the tail, turning around and sitting as close to one another as possible while facing the dim sky beyond the plane. Once the last man was situated, the interior went dark for a moment before illuminating us in a surreal red glow brought on by the flight lamps. The metal ramp in front of us closed, inching away our view of the night desert. It was accompanied by a long, high-pitched squeal that ended when it locked into place, encapsulating us in the aircraft. The low vibration inside the cabin heightened as the plane began taxiing to the runway, and then quieted once again as we slowed to a halt while waiting for takeoff.

Suddenly, the engines' hum increased to a fever pitch as they revved to full power, and our plane jolted and lurched forward down the runway. Our stomachs sank as the aircraft lifted off the ground and lined up with the other MC-130s banking north toward Iraq. The formation descended to avoid radar detection, and we began our flight two hundred feet above the desert.

Almost as soon as we crossed the border into Iraq, we began receiving enemy fire. The small windows over our heads glowed with the lightning flash of anti-aircraft tracers as our pilots dropped flares.

Two jumpmasters, posted at the jump door on either side of the aircraft, stood and yelled over the drone of the engines, "*TWENTY... MINUTES.*"

"Twenty minutes," the jumpers echoed.

One of the jumpmasters then yelled, "The Ranger Creed!"

Everyone in the cabin recited the familiar words in as much unison as the propeller noise would allow.

"*Recognizing that I volunteered as a Ranger, fully knowing the hazards of my chosen profession...*"

I basked in the anticipation of the mission to come, my thoughts drifting back to the crushing monotony of my life before the Army.

"I accept the fact that as a Ranger, my country expects me to move further, faster, and fight harder than any other soldier..."

During a history class on ancient Greece at the start of my freshman year of high school, the teacher asked who among us would want to grow up in Athens, and who in Sparta. I was the only one who raised a hand for Sparta. When my teacher asked why, I said, "Because they win." The rest of the class stared at me with a mixture of disinterest and disgust, except for a girl named Sarah.

"Energetically will I meet the enemies of my country. I shall defeat them on the field of battle for I am better trained and will fight with all my might..."

I spent the rest of high school sitting in the back of the class and reading paperbacks about special operations from Vietnam to Somalia. My best friend and I often skipped school for a week at a time to go hiking in the Smoky Mountains, and I counted down the days until I could join the Army. Within a week of graduation, I kissed Sarah goodbye and left for basic training.

"Surrender is not a Ranger word. I will never leave a fallen comrade to fall into the hands of the enemy..."

Near the end of infantry training, we emerged from our tents one morning to find our drill sergeants still inside the cadre building. We milled outside for an hour before a lone drill sergeant opened the door and asked, "Who has family in New York City?" A handful of privates raised their hands. "Do any of you have family members who work in the World Trade Center?" All hands went down except one. "Come with me," the drill sergeant said.

"Readily will I display the intestinal fortitude required to fight on to the Ranger objective and complete the mission, though I be the lone survivor."

I was now in my element, working with like-minded people who chose to go into harm's way. In Afghanistan, I discovered that I was good in a gunfight. I didn't get scared. Sudden enemy fire, raids into desolate compounds, long patrols through mountainous valleys—all of it had given me a laser-like focus that could last for hours. The first time Remy and I were almost killed by a Taliban rocket soaring a few feet over our heads and exploding nearby, we had laughed like children even as the blast's concussion knocked the wind from our lungs.

"*RANGERS LEAD THE WAY!*"

Beside their respective doors, the jumpmasters gave a final nod to one another before squaring off to face the jumpers. My thoughts returned to more immediate concerns. Once I had been rigged with parachute equipment, urination became impossible.

That was now over four hours ago.

"*TEN... MINUTES.*" In anticipation of the next command, we unclipped the safety line from the aircraft floor and stuffed the webbing and carabiner into an accessible pocket.

"*GET... READY.*"

A pause.

"*ALL PERSONNEL... STAND... UP.*"

Commotion ensued as we struggled to our feet to begin the ten excruciating minutes of standing before the lights beside each jump door would change from red to green.

"*HOOK... UP.*"

We unclipped the static line hook from our reserve parachute's carrying strap and snapped it onto the steel cable stretched over our heads.

"*CHECK... STATIC... LINES.*"

After inspecting the yellow length of my static line for tears from the hook-up point to where it disappeared over my shoulder, I proceeded to check Remington's line. The webbing snaked a predetermined distance back and forth behind his chute, which would automatically deploy once stretched taut as he dropped from the plane. Finding no issues, I tapped him on the helmet to let him know he was good.

"*CHECK... EQUIPMENT.*"

I ran my hand around my chin strap to ensure that I would not lose my helmet on exit, snapped my leg and chest straps to check that they were connected, and felt the lace holding the top of the weapon case on my side. My bladder felt like it was going to explode.

"*SOUND OFF FOR EQUIPMENT CHECK.*"

The signal started at the rear of the plane and passed like dominoes via a slap on the body and the word, "OKAY." I listened to Rangers yelling in succession from rear to front until I felt a hand smack my ribs, which I then relayed to Remington. The first jumper gave a final signal to the jumpmaster, who turned and slid his jump door upward and open. As the plane filled with the deafening roar of wind and turboprops, clouds of pale sand rolled inside. Rangers cheered as the jumpmasters began checking the jump doors. The familiar pain of standing uncomfortably with my parachute and full equipment began to grow.

"I have to pee so fucking bad," Remington shouted over his shoulder as we stood under the crushing weight of our gear.

"Me too."

The jumpmasters yelled something.

Remington asked, "Did they just say one minute?"

"I think so."

"*THIRTY... SECONDS.*"

"See you on the ground, Remy."

"Have a good jump, Slick."

I never saw the green light turn on or heard the command to "GO." Instead, the line of jumpers on the opposite side of the plane surged forward a moment before my row headed for the door. We shuffled forward, the noise of the engines and the shriek of the wind growing louder with each step. Deep, rhythmic whooshing noises accompanied each jumper's exit. Remington vanished out of the porthole and into the darkness. I handed my line to the safety, turned right to face the howl of the open door, and jumped into the black sky over Iraq.

3

August 19, 2007
Stewart International Airport, New York

I walked through the ground terminal's sliding glass doors, then stepped onto the sidewalk and squinted into the afternoon sun. A white passenger jet thundered low overhead on its final approach before vanishing over the building behind me. Smearing a hand over my unshaven face, I adjusted the strap of the ballistic nylon bag on my shoulder and wheeled my luggage to the curb.

A row of cars idled as fellow passengers found their loved ones. Removing my sunglasses from their perch atop my unkempt hair, I slid them over my eyes and watched half a dozen happy reunions. Beyond the cars, a slew of college-aged kids in West Point shirts and hats filed to a waiting shuttle bus. I checked the time on my phone, and had just pocketed it again when the decrepit pickup truck rolled into the waiting area.

I heard it before I saw it—a maroon Dodge Ram diesel with multiple impact pockmarks and damage to the body and paint that had gone unrepaired. The exposed metal had subsequently rusted under the eye of one or more of the three owners who had driven the truck before it found its way to the man currently sitting behind the wheel. The vehicle roared past me before the driver hit the brakes and swung into an open parking spot, then yelled, "Hurry up, cracker!" through the open passenger window.

I approached the truck from behind, seeing the New York license plate *321CYA* before I lowered the rickety tailgate and pulled off a blue tarp covering the contents in the back. After loading my single piece of checked luggage, I slung the bag from my back and gently set it beside a virtually identical stash bag bearing three or more times the number of red scrape marks as mine. Tucking the tarp around the bottom of the bags, I slammed the tailgate shut twice before it latched. I approached the passenger door, which creaked as I forced it open.

Jackson, a diminutive white man ten years my senior, stared back at me. His bushy blond hair and sideburns framed an oversized pair of aviator sunglasses.

He threw the floor shifter into first gear and said, "What happened to you, fucker? You look like shit. Get in."

I slid onto a cloth bench seat and closed the door behind me as the faithful pickup lurched forward, cutting off a car behind us and eliciting a long honk of objection. From the driver's seat, Jackson looked over at me while simultaneously steering with one hand knuckle-up on top of the wheel as the other hand worked the shifter.

"Got laid three times this weekend," he said matter-of-factly. "Didn't even have to use Craigslist. A new bar opened across the street from me on Friday, and blow is like catnip to these Spanish Harlem chicks. Tell them you've got coke back in the apartment and they walk right out the door with you."

I asked, "Isn't the coke more expensive than paying for whores in the first place?"

"Not with my dealer hookup. And, seriously, you look like you haven't slept in a week. Rough time back home, or what?"

I leaned my head against the seat, staring at the torn fabric on the ceiling. "Sarah and I broke up this weekend."

Jackson swung his head toward me, scanning my expression. The truck rolled over the rumble strips on the side of the road, and he veered back on course.

"Dude," he said. "I'm sorry. What happened?"

"She was sleeping with my best friend from back home."

"How do you know?"

"Because he said, 'Sarah and I have been sleeping together.'"

"But that's been falling apart for a while, right? You told me you weren't even sure if the wedding would happen. That was close to a year ago."

"Yeah. Well, now you can clear your calendar."

"Have you told anyone else yet?"

"No. But eventually I'm going to have to explain it to everyone I've met since age fifteen. And she has to tell her family, because they're all planning a wedding that won't happen next summer."

"I wasn't ready to be a best man, anyway. Look at it this way, cracker: you've got, what, ten months until you graduate?"

"Nine."

"Less than a year. Whatever. And if you graduate in 2008, then you'll be back in combat by 2009. It's not that far off."

"I never should have left in the first place."

We crossed onto the Newburgh-Beacon Bridge suspended a hundred feet over the water. I looked through steel girders at the broad expanse of the Hudson River stretching south; its rippling currents caught a million flashing sparkles from the sunset. My eyes danced across the darkening hilltops in front of us, looking for Ma Bell.

Jackson slapped a backhand across my arm. "Hey, fucker. If you hadn't left, you wouldn't have started skydiving. Or winning collegiate skydiving medals."

"That all got old after a few hundred jumps, Jackson."

"But if you hadn't lost the rush, you wouldn't have met me. And you wouldn't be going where we're about to go."

"That's true," I conceded.

He checked his watch. "And now you're only an hour away from the possibility of imminent death. That's not so bad, right?"

"No."

He nodded curtly. "Exactly. So chin up, David. The best is all ahead of us."

* * *

I quickly ascended the narrow metal ladder, the faint clanging of my boots on the thin rungs interspersed with the sounds of Jackson climbing below me. The weight of my nylon stash bag pressed against my back, and each current of wind washed chills over my sweat-soaked shirt as the temperature began plummeting from its balmy afternoon high into the sixties. The poles of the ladder disappeared into a man-sized gap in the red metal grating above me, and beyond it was only clear blue sky. I pressed my body to the ladder, but still felt the scrape of my stash bag against the platform's narrow opening as I pulled myself onto the pinnacle of Ma Bell.

The setting sun cast a subdued orange glow on the forested hilltops around us, and shadows pooled in the valleys between them. The rolling terrain gave way to the flat sapphire span of the Hudson River, whose far shore met West Point's tiny cluster of gray stone buildings. The sparkling twinkle of lights from Michie Stadium crowned the campus from an adjacent hill, now miles away and gleaming like a star.

Jackson stepped off the ladder and followed my gaze. "And no one at West Point knows you do this? Not even your skydiving team?"

"No way. That place kicks people out for cheating; I don't think felony trespassing would go over too well. What do you think about the winds? I'd put us at three to five knots out of the southwest, gusting to eight." I took the stash bag off my back, then set it on the ground and knelt beside it to open the drawstring.

"Gusting to ten, at least," he replied, taking off his own stash bag. "Still better than last time in the city."

I pulled a parachute container from my bag and began inspecting my gear. "Speaking of that," I said, "I've got a three-day pass coming up for Labor Day. What do you think about working our way around the Bronx? I need more building experience."

Jackson ignored me, instead checking his own parachute before pulling the harness over his shoulders. I did the same, then stepped through the leg straps before attaching the chest strap and tightening the webbing. Once we were finished, we folded our stash bags and stuffed them into our cargo pockets.

"Let me check you out," he said, performing a quick walk-around inspection of my parachute. "You're good. Do mine."

"Why aren't you answering me about Labor Day?"

"Hurry up and check. I'm getting cold."

I examined his harness from front to back, ending my inspection with a slap on his shoulder. "You're good. So what about Labor Day weekend?"

He turned to face me. "You've got to have some normal college kid things you can do."

"Fuck no. My roommate is taking some guys home to Philly, but I told them I had to skydive, so I'm totally free."

"Well, go back and tell them you'd love to go."

"Why? If you're busy I can still come here to Ma Bell by myself, or see if Nick can meet up and—"

"David, you and your fiancée just broke up. Go to Philly and get drunk with your friends. Chase skirts. Be a college kid for a few days."

"I can get drunk with you."

"All your free time is spent hanging out with adrenaline junkies, and the truth is we're all as fucked up in the head as you are. You need a break. I've been right before, and I'm right about this. Do I need to remind you about the loops?"

My jaw set. "No."

"Let's discuss the loops for a minute—"

"Fine, goddammit. I'll go to Philly and waste my time drinking beer and listening to kids talk about sports."

"Good. Three."

"But the weekend after that you have to take me to the World's Fair towers in Queens."

"Fine. Two."

"Maybe as a part of a Harlem River tower doubleheader."

"Don't push it. One."

"See you on the ground, Jackson."

"See ya." He turned and took three blindingly fast steps before leaping off the edge of the platform.

He fell for one second before reaching back and throwing his pilot chute. It immediately inflated, pulling on the long bridle that extracted the canopy from the container. With a loud crack, his main parachute exploded open into a clean, black rectangle, and Jackson soared beneath it in a hard, carving right turn back to the landing area. He lined up with the narrow length of grass we had crossed after leaving the woods, then touched down and pulled his parachute to the ground.

I walked to the platform's edge.

The tips of my boots hovered over oblivion, and I stood in silence to let the fear wash over me in waves. Alone amidst the framework of the windswept antenna, and high above the painful realities of my life that I had left on the ground when I began climbing, I had found the only place in the world where I could clear my head. A hundred mental battles of the day were laid to rest in that solitary environment. There was no Sarah, no affair on the top platform of Ma Bell; my mind focused solely on its very existence, and possibly its end.

I took a final breath. "Three... two... one... see ya," I said, jumping off the edge.

A fatal fall unfolded as I plunged into the void, my speed increasing as treetops raced toward me. My senses were on fire, my mind and body screaming that death was imminent. I hit the end of a one-second count before reaching back to grasp my pilot chute. I let another long second and a half pass before throwing it to the side. The height of the trees intensified the ground rush, presenting the impression that impact was inevitable before my parachute burst open, jerking me upright as I grabbed the steering toggles.

A slight tailwind pushed me over the trees and away from the open field as I banked into a hard right turn. After lining up with my intended touch-down point, I descended toward Jackson's figure. Pulling the toggles down to shoulder level, I bled off altitude, and the whistle of wind in my ears quieted as I slowed. Transitioning to a flare, I lowered my hands to my waist as the ground approached, and I touched down softly a few feet from Jackson before collapsing my parachute.

Jackson was undoing his chest strap from the buckle and looking at me with a raised eyebrow. "You're starting to take it pretty low out here, fucker. Remember that if you bounce, I've got to deal with it."

I looked up at Ma Bell. The massive, four-sided framework of alter-nating red and white metal beams rose into the crystalline blue sky, tapering as it ascended into the square platform hovering 360 feet overhead. A broad smile crossed my face as the lingering surge of adrenaline infused with the overwhelming euphoria of a safe touchdown; BASE jumping was like killing yourself and walking away, death and resurrection combined in those precious few seconds that made everything else in life bearable.

He was still watching me, waiting for a response.

"That's true, Jackson. But we all have to be selfish every once in a while."

4

September 1, 2007
Devon, Pennsylvania

I awoke in the darkness, like always.

No dreams, no sudden startles at real or perceived noises like a normal war vet, though I couldn't remember waking up like that before my tours in Afghanistan and Iraq—just wide awake in a split second, fully alert and conscious. The abrupt wake-ups were only my second most noticeable memento of combat, the first being a constant ringing in my ears like a shrill, high-pitched dial tone on each side of my head that accompanied permanent hearing loss. As I listened through the ringing, I heard a low, repetitive sound that I eventually recognized as snoring.

I sat up on the air mattress, my eyes adjusting to the two other bodies in the room. One slept on the lone bed, the other on a second air mattress. Pulling a thin blanket off my waist, I rose and felt my way along the wall to the backpack that doubled as my survival kit for the inevitable. Picking it up and swinging the strap over my shoulder, I opened the door and crept out of the room.

I stepped into the hallway and looked across the railing to a second floor foyer window that rose eight feet above the front door. Beyond it, rows of affluent houses lined the wide street of the Philadelphia subdivision, and ground lights illuminated fragments of neatly trimmed shrubs and swimming pools. Following the railing past an open bathroom and several more closed doors, I turned and descended the stairs barefoot.

Walking past the front door, I slipped through a dark entryway and felt around for the kitchen light switch.

I retrieved a glass from a cabinet next to the sink and filled it a third of the way with ice cubes before setting my bag on the floor and taking a seat at the dining room table. I withdrew my laptop and powered it on, then removed a bottle of Woodford Reserve, opened it, and poured three inches of bourbon. I didn't bother replacing the cork.

Opening a blank Word document on the laptop, I watched the black cursor blink against a bright white screen. I lifted the glass to my face with a light whirl to circulate the bourbon around the ice, breathing in fragrant notes of spice and vanilla before taking a long drink. Then I settled my fingertips over the keys.

Suddenly, I heard a keychain rattle outside the front door, followed by the flat *clack* of a deadbolt turning. Pushing back my chair, I stood and walked into the foyer in time to see the door open. A single figure stood silhouetted in the ambient light.

"And who are you, exactly?" she asked.

I stalled for a moment. The girl was dressed in a loose Ohio State shirt over sweatpants that ended in a pair of fur-lined moccasins. The strap of one duffel bag neatly divided the shirt between her breasts, and she held another duffel in one hand as she pocketed her keys.

"I'm a friend of your brother's."

"Oh, of course. I'm sorry. I've been driving since four o'clock. Holiday traffic was terrible."

"In your defense, this could be a really elaborate home robbery ruse." I reached forward and took the duffel from her hand. "Let me help you with your bags."

"I can get them."

"No. Come on."

She blew a wisp of straw-blonde hair out of her face before unslinging the other duffel and handing it to me. As I hefted the strap over my shoulder, she swept her hair back with cupped fingers and straightened her posture.

"I'm Laila," she said.

"David. Where do you want these?"

"My room's upstairs. Thanks." She locked the door behind her and led the way toward the steps, stopping at the dining room entryway. "What's going on over there?"

I looked at my open laptop and bourbon. "Homework."

"At one in the morning, while drinking?"

"That's how I do my best thinking."

"Where are your books?"

I tapped the side of my head with two fingers. "All up here."

She shrugged indifferently, and we walked up the stairs.

"This is me," she said, opening a door and stepping aside.

I set her bags on the bedroom floor, glancing at the stuffed animals arranged on her tidy bed under a high school pennant. On the dresser, a wide cloth frame held a photo of teenage girls in green track shorts with their arms around one another. I stepped back out of the room.

She studied me with her clear green eyes. "So is everyone else already passed out? I thought you guys would still be burning it down by now."

"We started early," I said.

"None of you would survive at Ohio State, you know."

"I know. Not a lot of legal drinking opportunities at West Point."

"So why are you still going?"

"I said, not a lot of 'legal' opportunities."

"Wait—you're Steve's roommate, aren't you?"

"I am."

"So you're the elusive Rivers, the one who hides all your booze in the cadet room."

"Yeah, I guess."

She gave a quick laugh. "He's told me a lot about you."

"Like what?"

"That you shot a bunch of people overseas and you don't give a shit about West Point. And you spend all your time jumping out of helicopters. True?"

"Not entirely. I jump out of planes, too."

Her phone chimed. She slid it from her pocket and checked the display. "Oh, it's Peter. I was supposed to call him when I got here. I have to go."

"Peter?"

"My boyfriend. I have to go."

"Of course. Goodnight, Laila."

"Goodnight, Rivers."

I returned to the dining room and sat down to write, but the words didn't come. Sitting back in the chair, I drank my glass of bourbon and poured another, then leaned forward and rested my fingers over the keys once more. The cursor continued to blink at me, awaiting my guidance to begin its dutiful march across the screen, leaving a trail of letters in its wake.

One hour and two more glasses of bourbon later, the words still wouldn't come.

I heard footsteps descending the stairs before Laila appeared in the entryway. "How's the homework going?" she asked.

"Not well. You interrupted my flow."

"If it makes you feel better, I can't sleep. Too much coffee on the drive, I suppose."

I nodded toward the bottle of Woodford. "I'll buy you a drink."

"Peter would love that."

"Your secret's safe with me. Come on now, Buckeye. Show me how Ohio State girls do it."

She gave a rueful smile of concession, but said nothing as she retrieved a glass from the kitchen, filled it with ice, and sat across from me. She poured herself a double and raised her glass.

"To secrets," I said, tapping my glass against hers. We both took a sip.

"I'm surprised you came home with Steve. He said he always offers and you never take him up on it."

"I usually stay pretty busy."

"Trying to get college girls drunk?"

"If I'm being honest, you're the first."

"Really? As a senior?"

"Really."

"I find that hard to believe."

I sighed, staring at the bourbon remaining in my glass. "Up until a few weeks ago, I had a fiancée I'd been loyal to for eight years. Then I found out she'd been sleeping with my best friend since I joined the Army. Now I spend most nights BASE jumping. So to be honest, I couldn't care less about the college girls."

"What is BASE jumping?"

"It means I spend most of my time sneaking around in the dark and breaking into buildings or finding antennas to jump off of. I've had to run from the cops, and I've almost been killed a couple of times. Got arrested jumping a waterfall and barely kept my school from finding out. Had a bad opening and flew into the side of the antenna a few weeks ago, and had to climb a hundred feet on the outside framework to recover my parachute. That's BASE jumping."

"Does my brother know you do that?"

"No. No one does."

"Why are you telling me?"

"I don't know."

She nodded. "Well, you're not the only one with issues. I'm sure you know about my dad."

"No."

"Steve never told you?"

"Steve doesn't talk about his family all that much, to tell you the truth."

"We had a townhouse when my dad worked at McKinsey. He had this home office at the top of the stairs that he usually kept locked. But sometimes he'd forget. And whenever he did, Steve and I would sneak in there before he came home from work. He had all this cool stuff from his travels around the world. African masks, these really ornate painted elephants from India, stuff like that. And we could sit in this old, leather-bound rolling chair he loved, and spin around and look at everything.

"Well, one day Steve got sent home from school before my mom got back. So he went up the stairs and checked the office door, and it's unlocked, so he went in. And my dad was sitting in his chair, facing the door. And he had... he had shot himself with a revolver that my mom thought he'd sold when she got pregnant with Steve."

"I'm sorry," I said. "I didn't know."

"We went to family counseling, which helped a little. But in a way, the hardest part about everything wasn't losing him."

"What was?"

"The hardest part," she said, her fingers toying with the glass of bourbon as she stared vacantly at the table, "was that we never knew why he did it. There was nothing wrong between him and my mom, nothing at work. I mean, we weren't rich, but they were doing fine. We never found out anything. He just... left."

Her phone chimed. "It's Peter again," she said, checking it. "He's on Illinois time, so when he stays out drinking I get calls an hour later than I should. The joys of a long-distance relationship."

"Just pretend you're asleep," I offered.

She looked at me under raised eyebrows. "He's jealous enough as it is. No need to rile him up."

I raised my bourbon. "Thanks for drinking with me."

She lifted her glass and clinked it against mine. "To secrets."

After taking a final sip, she rose and walked around the corner. I watched her glass across the table, listening as her footsteps receded before ending altogether with the sound of a door closing above me.

5

February 22, 2008
Garrison, New York

I pushed open the door and Laila rushed inside to get out of the cold, tossing her purse onto the unmade bed. Locking the door behind me, I set the key card on the side table and looked up to see her removing her coat to reveal a deep violet dress that ended at her knees, exposing calves toned from frequent running.

She asked, "What are you looking at, Rivers?"

"Just enjoying the view."

"The balcony is over there if you need a view. You're just objectifying me."

I walked to the sliding glass door and gestured to the eerily bright moon that shone across a clear black sky. "Gala ball, luxurious hotel accommodations, and a full moon... I'm not doing so bad as a boyfriend, am I?"

She sat on the mattress and leaned down to unfasten the straps of her heels, exposing a generous portion of cleavage. Her electric green eyes watched me as she took off one heel, then the other.

"What can I say?" she answered. "If we weren't already sleeping together, tonight would be the night."

"And look at the bright side," I added. "That's one less West Point banquet we have to go to."

"Your school does love its formal events. You know what we do at Ohio State when the seniors have a hundred nights until graduation?"

"No, what?"

"Nothing. But you guys turn it into a three-ring circus with distinguished speakers and everything else." She stood and turned away from me, then looked back over her shoulder. "Now unzip me, Cadet Rivers."

"Gladly." I stepped forward and pulled the zipper down the small of her back, breathing in an intoxicating mix of hairspray and perfume as I slid the straps off her slim shoulders and kissed her neck.

She leaned her head back, resting a cascade of curled blonde hair against my shoulder and looking up at me between dark eyelashes. "Do you need help taking off your nutcracker jacket?"

I looked down at the thick, wool uniform top that was lined with three vertical rows of brass buttons under a short, stiff collar.

"They call it Full Dress Gray. And no."

"I like my name better."

I placed my lips next to her ear and whispered, "Just because it's more accurate doesn't make it right."

The sound of her phone ringing interrupted the moment.

"Shit," she said with a sigh, "it's probably Mom."

"Why is she calling at midnight?"

"I don't know." She hastily pulled a single strap over her shoulder with one hand while reaching for her purse with the other. Fishing out her phone, she looked at the display and froze.

"What the fuck do you want?" she said, bringing the phone to her ear.

Then she stood perfectly still for ten seconds. Fifteen.

I stepped forward and rested a palm on her shoulder, but she flung her arm back to throw it off.

"Fuck you," she said into the phone receiver. "You were the worst mistake I ever made, you piece of shit." Then she threw the phone against the mattress and pressed herself into my arms, sobbing.

"It was him," she cried.

"What did he say?"

"He's drunk. But he said…" She trailed off into tears.

"He said what?"

"He said Dad killed himself because he was ashamed of me, and that he was burning in hell—"

"Babe, I'm sorry."

"I just—I need a minute, David."

"Take all the time you need."

She pushed away from my chest and went into the bathroom, closing the door behind her. I listened to her sobs as I walked to the bed and picked up her phone, then entered the number of the last call into my own phone before turning hers off and setting it back down on the disheveled comforter.

Then I walked toward the sliding glass door and stepped into the frigid night, pulling the door shut behind me and casting another glance at the bathroom before dialing. I walked across a thick carpet of undisturbed snow to the balcony railing, waiting for him to pick up as I looked across treetops that ended below a stretch of gleaming Hudson River punctuating rolling hills, the entire landscape shrouded in white and glowing under the moon. The line connected after three rings.

An intoxicated voice said, "Who's this?"

"Hello, Peter. I'm David Rivers."

"What's up, douchebag? Figured I might be hearing from you."

"You figured right."

"Is this where you threaten me?"

"Why would I threaten you, Peter?"

"Because you don't want me calling your bitch. But I had her first."

"She's changing her number tomorrow. But I'm not. And I promise you, Peter"—I reached up to my throat with a thumb and forefinger to pinch open the stiff uniform collar—"you can call me anytime you like."

"You sound like a faggot. Tell that whore her dad got what he deserved."

"Because he killed himself?"

"Like a fucking coward."

"Peter, after what's happening here tonight, I think you should strongly consider that option yourself."

"You don't know me, pussy."

"I'm starting to get a pretty good idea. Killing yourself would be the most honorable thing you can do."

"No, that would be beating your fucking ass like you deserve for stealing my bitch. But I'm over it."

"Are you?"

"You know what? Fuck you. Have fun with the whore, and tell her she's never going to forget me because I was the best she ever had."

"I don't think I'll forget you either, Peter."

"Whatever, douchebag. You think I'm scared of you? You want to meet me like a man, I'll give you the address. But I've got guns, and my friends have guns, too, so if you come out to Illinois, tread lightly."

He hung up.

I placed the phone in my pocket, inhaling sharply. Then I released a long, slow breath into the freezing air around me, watching it turn into a cloud that, for a fleeting moment, blocked the distant hills from view.

6

April 6, 2008
Garrison, New York

I crossed the parking lot through a light drizzle, glancing beyond the fence to where the terrain dropped off toward the water. On a clear day, the view would have extended all the way to Storm King Mountain, but a thick blanket of morning fog hovered over the landscape, revealing only intermittent glimpses of vibrant green trees beneath a sky the color of shale rock.

Walking under an overhang, I passed three doors before stopping at our room. I passed the cardboard tray holding two large cups of coffee to my left hand and slid my right into my pocket, fumbling for the key card. I inserted it into the slot, pushed open the door, and stepped inside.

Laila was facing away from me, zipping her duffel bag on the bed.

"You're up early," I said, tossing the key card onto the side table and setting down the tray of coffee. "We don't have to check out until noon."

She turned to face me, her eyes teary and bloodshot.

"What happened?"

"This is what you've been doing after I go to sleep, David?" She jabbed a finger toward the corner of the room, and I saw my laptop open on the desk. "You told me you were doing fucking homework!"

"Laila, I don't know what you read but—"

"There's close to a hundred pages there, David. Half are about almost killing yourself with a parachute, and the other half are about wanting to kill yourself with a gun."

I walked toward her, but she threw out her hands. "Don't fucking touch me, David. I can't handle this after my dad. I can't handle it."

"I never meant for you to read that."

"That's all you have to say? Do you know what it's like when someone you love takes his own life?"

"I wish you hadn't gone through my computer, Laila."

"We're done, David." She grabbed her duffel and strode past me toward the door.

I whirled around to face her and yelled, "You think I want to be this way? You think I asked for this? That I don't want to be normal? I didn't get to choose, and there's not a goddamn thing I can do except write about it. You think I don't know how this ends for me?"

"We all get a choice, David," she whispered. "But I'm not going to be here when you make the wrong one."

Then she turned and walked out the door, letting it slam shut behind her.

I took a deep, surging breath and held it as I raked a hand across my scalp, then made a fist and slowly exhaled. I lowered my hand, walked to the desk, and sat across from the computer. The cursor was still blinking at my last entry from the night before.

It always angers me to hear people talk about suicide being a selfish act.

Here is what it's like: you're locked in a telephone booth with a huge man who is endlessly dragging his nails across a chalkboard, the shrill sounds choking out everything else and making your blood curl, driving your mind to the breaking point. You can't plug your ears, you can't tell him to stop; he is a deaf blind mute and he's not going to quit unless you make him. Just as you're cocking your fist back to punch him in the face, family members, well-wishers, and pundits from the street run up the sidewalk and pound on the soundproof glass of the phone booth, screaming, "DON'T HIT HIM! That would be a selfish act!"

You're goddamn right it would be a selfish act. What else would it be? Why else would you do it—for someone else's approval? Who are these people to tell you what not to do, when they have no idea what you're hearing? They—them, the rest of the world; it's completely irrelevant whether they are biologically related or not—are going about their happy lives, content with their TV and their social media, on their way to the house or the office. Those people on the outside have never been trapped in the booth. They have no idea what you're hearing, what fills your mind every passing second against your will, and they're trying to pass judgment on you because your act will negatively affect their happy lives— they might miss a sitcom over it, they might be unable to sleep. How dare you inconvenience them?

What about your family? Family has nothing to do with it. They're not in the phone booth; they're outside in the open air and peaceful tranquility and sunshine. They may think they can understand what you're hearing because they can see you through the glass, but they don't. They've never been inside the booth, and they never will. Occasionally, one of those people on the outside will make some attempt at suicide. They will statistically regret it at some point in the process, and far more of them survive than die. If they live, they will spend the rest of their lives talking about "how close they came." They will feel like they've been given a second chance, they will thank a god of their choice for their newfound strength. They have never been in the booth, either.

But the passers-by on the street will point to them and say, through the glass, "See? See how selfish that was? We could have helped them cope with that difficult issue if only they'd TALKED TO US!"

The people who have been in the booth, trapped in the enclosed space with that horrible noise, who have cocked their fist, if only for a moment, even if they haven't thrown that punch yet and even if they never will, have an understanding with each other. They may never speak it, and their families—the ones they're supposed to not throw that punch for—probably have no fucking idea they're even in the booth in the first place.

The truth is, it would and should be a selfish act. Because no one on the outside hears what you're hearing and understands why you want to punch this guy in the face to make him stop. Every significant choice in life is a selfish act, so why not in death?

If you haven't experienced it, you will never understand. If you have, you will.

It's that simple. That is the price of being able to describe it—you have to experience it. It is like drug users getting high in order to see the other side. They pay the money and endure the medical and legal risks to catch a glimpse of it. Except, with the darkness, the glimpse you catch isn't euphoria or bliss or hallucinogenic inspiration—the other side you see is a terrible, dark, twisted world, and you can't get out. You didn't even choose to go in the first place. You did nothing different, but your surroundings started to look a little more distorted each morning, and then one day you woke up and you were there.

Drug users come out of their journey knowing what an acid trip or a heroin binge feels like. People with the darkness come out being able to write descriptions of the things they saw and felt, things they couldn't possibly have begun to imagine had they not been there. Or, they might not come out at all. They might never leave. Even though you never wanted it, the darkness is addictive; it is a drug that chooses you.

The darkness is very hard to break and will most likely require an intervention from the outside, although in most cases the "intervention" doesn't know it's intervening—it might just be accidentally providing a distraction. The intervention may be a person or an event, and you don't have the power to summon it. It might come and it might not; you might be saved and you might not.

Some return to the outside world and can speak of what they felt inside the booth, and some never return at all.

* * *

Jackson set his beer on the table between us and glanced out the window toward the Hudson River marina that was obscured by rain in the evening twilight. Other drinkers had just begun flowing into the Front Street Bar in Newburgh, though Jackson and I were on our third round before the house lights dimmed in anticipation of the post-dinner influx of customers.

"It's not that fucking bad, man," he said over the classic rock blaring from ceiling speakers.

"Jackson, she was perfect."

He waited for a laughing couple to pass our table before responding, "How long until you graduate?"

"A month. You know that."

"And how long will your next deployment to Iraq or Afghanistan last?"

"A year. Maybe more."

"You think a girl like that is going to stick around? For someone like us?"

"Probably not, but—"

"If she hadn't read your shit today, she would've done it eventually. Valerie got into my emails by hacking my password with a program she bought for forty bucks. You have any idea how graphic my emails are? With how many women?"

I pushed my bourbon aside. "I never cheated on Laila."

"No, you're just a suicidal, alcoholic writer. That's probably worse."

"She didn't know that."

"I'm not knocking it, man. Welcome to the machine. Neither of us wants to grow old, and neither of us will. Stop stressing over it. You might bounce on our next jump, anyway."

"Let's do the power tower tonight."

"Even if the winds weren't too high, which they are, it's pouring outside."

"The rain is supposed to stop later."

"Look, I'm not trying to tell you what to do. I don't know much about electrical arcing, so I should probably do some research, but you want to climb next to 470,000 volt live wires in heavy precipitation with no moon? Maybe it's better to wait."

"I bet Nick would do it with me."

"Gay Nick or Cowboy Nick?"

"Cowboy Nick."

"He's leaving for a Norway trip tomorrow. Good luck."

"Drew, then."

"His canopy is still being repaired from the church jump."

"We could do Ma Bell—"

"David, do you remember the last time you didn't listen to me?"

I turned to look at the aquarium stretching the length of the bar, the fish and coral shifting color under the tank's undulating lights. "No."

"Not only are you not always right, you're usually wrong."

"You can't bring up the loops every time you want to make a point."

"I can, and I will," he said defiantly. "I told you to loosen the closing loops on your BASE rig so you wouldn't have a pilot chute in tow. But you wanted to listen to your precious manufacturer recommendations."

"All I knew about you at the time was that your financial portfolio consisted of cocaine and prostitutes. Of course I listened to the manufacturer—"

"And then on the Harlem River tower, you almost towed into the fucking ground before your chute opened. I turned to Ryan and said, 'Dude, he's going in,' and had time to say it before your pins popped."

"The loops were a mistake," I shot back. "We've discussed this."

"You were allowed to be pissed about Sarah because you'd been with her for eight years. How long were you with Laila, eight months?"

"You saw her, Jackson. She was perfect."

"But we're not. I've been around a few more years than you. Get used to this. With as much as we jump and the risks we take, just finding someone who will fuck you regularly for a few months at a time is a victory. You remember how I kept blowing you off after you got back from your first BASE jump course a couple years ago?"

"Yeah."

"I thought you'd lose your drive to do it until you bothered me to the point that you were about to start climbing shit and jumping on your own. Know why I took you out to Ma Bell the first time?"

"Because you cared about my emotional well-being?"

"Fuck no. I didn't know who you were and didn't give a shit. But you were going to bounce at some point doing a local object on your own, and end up burning it for the rest of us. That's your problem—you're persistent about things even when you shouldn't be. You're in a school you hate because they said you couldn't go there when you first applied. You didn't leave Sarah, even when she turned into a fucking cunt and started treating you like shit. And let's tell the truth—that happened a long time before you found out she cheated on you. Can you blame her? You'd been seeing her once every few months for almost five years. And now you're clinging to the memory of a girl who literally ran out the door the second she found out who you are. Let her go, man."

"I'm just fucking broken right now, Jackson."

"We both are." He slid a hand across the back of his neck and then straightened in his seat, his forceful stare upon me. "Let her go."

7

I pushed open the glass door and stepped into the colossal lobby of the Association of Graduates building. A sunroof in the high ceiling shone natural light over a marble floor lined with walls bearing framed West Point prints of every variety: cadets marching in step, gray stone buildings, a freeze-frame of uniform caps suspended in midair over a graduating class, and cadet portraits of alumni who had gone on to the general officer ranks, the presidency, or both. Lee, Grant, Eisenhower, Patton, MacArthur, Schwarzkopf, and a slew of others I didn't recognize gazed hollowly upon me as I came to a stop in the center of the room.

"What can I help you with, son?"

I turned to see a broad-shouldered man with immaculate silver hair approaching me. He wore a navy blazer with a nametag bearing the subscript, *Colonel, Retired.*

I cleared my throat. "I just found out I'm getting kicked out of the Army, and I don't have a job."

"I see." He nodded. "What happened, if you don't mind my asking?"

"The EKG results from my commissioning physical just came back. They diagnosed me with supraventricular tachycardia."

"What is that?"

"I stopped listening after they said I was medically non-commissionable."

"And you're graduating with your class in a couple weeks?"

"Yes, sir."

"Not to worry, son. We'll get you straightened out. Let's go to my office."

I followed him down the hall and into a room decorated like the lobby, albeit with scattered pictures of an infantry platoon in Vietnam. I took a seat across from his desk.

"Are you an engineering major?" he asked.

"No."

He frowned. "Telecomm and corporate sales are pretty hot right now. We've also seen a rise in manufacturing and logistics hires as of late." He began sliding papers across his desk. "You can fill out this questionnaire to rank order your career field and geographical preferences. Also, here's a guide to creating your résumé. Once you get all of this done, bring it back with a copy of your transcript and we'll help you get everything in order before the next hiring conference."

"Thank you."

"You'll have to dress the part, obviously. Do you have a good suit?"

"No."

"Of course not. You've been wearing cadet gray. I'd recommend either navy or charcoal, and pinstripes always go over well at interviews. Make sure the leather on your shoes and belt matches. Antonello is the best tailor in the Cadet Store—ask for him by name, and tell him I sent you."

"Outstanding."

"And, son," he lowered his voice, "this can be a difficult transition when you've been expecting to be a lieutenant for so long. But remember, you're still part of the Long Gray Line. No one can ever take that away from you."

I angled my head to the side and felt my neck crack. "No, they can't take that away. Sir, thank you. This has been incredibly helpful."

We shook hands and I stood, neatly stacking the papers and taking them with me. As I passed through the lobby, my phone began to ring. When I saw that it was Jackson, I dumped the papers into a nearby wastebasket and stepped outside to answer.

"Are you ready for this?" I said. "I'm getting kicked out of the Army because of a non-terminal medical condition, so the past five years have been for nothing. You want to jump up here or do you want me to come to the city, because if I don't get a BASE fix there's not enough alcohol in the world to drown this one."

An unknown and tentative voice asked, "Uh... is this David?"

Fuck.

"Yes," I answered. "This is David."

"I'm Jackson's brother-in-law. He asked me to call you. He was in a motorcycle accident this morning."

"What happened?"

"He didn't remember much, but the police said he was hit by a car that ran a stop sign. He asked me to call you and Andrea, the girl he was supposed to go out with tonight."

"Sounds about right."

"Well, there are four different Andreas on his phone."

"Call them all. Which hospital is he at? I'll be down there in two hours."

"David, Jackson passed about an hour ago."

"He... passed?"

"He's dead."

I paused. "When will his services be?"

"They're working that out now. I'll let you know."

"Okay."

"And David?"

"Yes."

"He said everything would be okay, and not to forget the loops. He was adamant that I tell you that. Everything will be okay, and don't forget the loops."

* * *

It used to be nothing more than a novelty thought, an occasional glance into what it would be like. Then I found my mind continually drifting back to that gleaming silver revolver—first dozens of times a day, then hundreds. Now, it's a natural mental turn at the end of each thought. The symbol that came out of nowhere one day, a perfect vision of the barrel of a .454 revolver sliding into my mouth.

Flawless. Unprovoked. Why that gun, that caliber, that finish? I have no answers, only thoughts. They swarm into my mind like bats flapping into the crevices of a dark space, filling every void as soon as a distraction isn't there to push them out.

Perhaps my clouded mind, growing increasingly serious about its own annihilation, has simply presented me with its weapon of choice.

Who am I to deny it? Things have been getting perpetually worse for years. Every few months, there's a new plateau lower than the last. Each night turns into a sudden wake-up in the darkness, and I open my eyes in a gray, hollow room. Alone. My whole life is encompassed in this setting, one way or another. Am I in a barracks room at West Point, in a dark tent nestled in the mountains of Afghanistan, on the couch at Jackson's apartment? Only opening my eyes will tell me. Surroundings, the placement of objects in my immediate vicinity, distinguish that for me. The rest is the same.

That gray, hollow room of my mind, aware that I'm not asleep and on a bed, a couch, a cot, awake but not really awake, wanting to be one or the other but getting neither. I occupy the same gray, vacant space that I've found myself sitting in, lying in, standing in, at various hours of the night or morning—my whole life —alone. I don't need to open my eyes to know that. My stomach is nauseated. I want to either throw up or not feel sick, but I can't. The purgatory in between has set in like the space between being tired and falling asleep, the fog that I slide my feet through with my hands outstretched, not sure what I'll run into and finding out there's nothing.

There is no return from where I've been going ever since the war, combat that I have been banished from by yet another arrow of fate, another meaningless blow to increase the bleeding. Drinking more, eating and sleeping less as the emptiness is replaced by a darkness that grows inside me, the emptiness replaced by something worse.

Once only an inconvenience, being alive has now become the outright denial of a death sentence for a crime that I deserve to hang for, and not killing myself is a coward's way out that I have shamefully continued to take despite every possible indication that I shouldn't. I hate the liquor even as I drink it, knowing it has done nothing but delayed the inevitable through an illusion of normalcy, and yet I keep embracing the façade of comfort rather than feel reality as it is, find it unacceptable, and remove myself from its boundaries forever. It's a hollow substi-

tute of the same: the bottle a gun and alcohol a bullet, pouring it into my head to end it for now.

My cell phone rang on the desk beside me.

I stopped typing and leaned back in my chair. The glowing phone pierced the darkness that outlined the crisp, white rectangle of my computer screen. Pushing my glass aside, I reached for the phone.

A low voice said, "How's my bitch doing, faggot?"

"Peter," I replied. "You haven't killed yourself yet. How have you been?"

"Didn't think you'd be hearing from me again, did you?"

"To be honest, I'd almost forgotten about you entirely."

"Well I haven't forgotten about you, David River."

"Rivers."

"Whatever, douchebag. It doesn't matter, anyway, because I'm talking to a dead man."

"You are?" I leaned forward and propped my elbows on the desk.

"Yeah. I am."

"Sure you're not talking to someone who's going to teach you a lesson about fucking with people you don't know?"

"You stole my bitch, and now you're going to get what's coming to you."

"What's coming to me, Peter?"

"Revenge, motherfucker. I've got a bunch of friends who want to meet you."

"You sound drunk. Are you going to remember this tomorrow?"

"We're going to find your ass."

"Peter, you really should kill yourself. This is getting embarrassing."

"Fuck you."

"I recommend doing it while you're drunk so you end on a high note."

"It's going to happen soon, David. I'm coming for you."

I leaned back in my chair, smoothing my shirtfront and crossing an ankle over the opposite knee. "Peter, I'm glad you called. You couldn't have picked a better time."

* * *

"Cadet David Rivers."

Walking across the stage as the voice over the loudspeaker called the next name, I shook hands with one general, and then another, and then some political authority who handed me a cardboard tube encasing a diploma. After descending the steps on the far side, I stepped onto the artificial turf of the field and turned to see the interior of Michie Stadium, brightly lit under a cloudless sky. The bleachers were packed with civilians in colorful clothing and rose around a focal point of seated cadets dressed, as I was, in white pants and gray dress tops that were neatly divided at the waist by a maroon sash. I marched along with the procession of diploma-carrying graduates to my front, each of them ecstatically waving at family members in the crowd.

Returning to my seat, I waited for the remainder of the class to receive their diplomas. More formalities were spoken, culminating in a single cadet taking center stage.

"Class dismissed!" he shouted. Everyone around me threw their hats into the air and began cheering wildly. I stayed in my seat, my eyes locked in front of me as classmates embraced each other amid the hats crashing down on top of them. A moment later, small children came scrambling over the chairs like gremlins, trying to collect cadet hats in search of the traditional cash hidden inside.

Family and friends poured onto the field to find their proud new graduate, to celebrate their moment of great triumph. I took off my hat and dropped it onto the ground, then rose to leave.

Laila walked up to me. She was wearing a thin sundress that wrapped around her body. She was too nice to let me leave alone.

"Hey, David," she said.

"Hey, Laila."

"I'm sorry to hear you couldn't stay in the Army. Do you have any job interviews lined up?"

"No."

"So what are you going to do now?"

"Start over."

"Well, let me know if you need help, because my cousin started working for—"

"I appreciate it, Laila, but I'm going to be just fine."

She looked past me, and then locked her green eyes with mine. "Do you have anyone here for graduation?"

"No. One of the many joys of growing up in the foster system."

"What about Jackson?"

"Jackson's dead."

"Oh my God, I'm so sorry—"

"Laila." I put my hand on her shoulder. "I appreciate the concern. And I love you. I wish you all the happiness in the world, I really do. But right now, I've got to get the fuck out of here."

I kissed her, and her eyes began tearing up. I turned and walked away, crossing to the edge of the field and entering a concrete doorway, where I deposited my diploma in a trash can. As I ascended the stairs to the upper decks of the stadium, the newly-minted sophomore class was coming down.

"Congratulations, sir!" they called.

"Thank you, kids," I replied, arriving at the first landing and continuing to climb. Eventually I reached the top, emerging into the sunlight on the upper bleachers. Some of the new sophomores lingered in their seats.

A young black cadet asked, "Don't you need to change into Class A's before your commissioning ceremony?"

"I'm not commissioning," I said. "Medical."

"Oh, shit, I'm sorry."

"It's going to be okay, brother."

I climbed the outside stairs between benches until I reached the top rail, then leaned against it and faced east as a warm breeze washed over my face. Michie Stadium was surrounded by gray stone buildings, and the ground dropped sharply toward the gleaming, choppy Hudson River. Past the far shore, rolling green hills rose out of the water and extended for miles into the distance. Beyond the closest peaks, scattered hilltops emerged along the horizon. On one of them, a red and white antenna blinked.

I sighed, watching Ma Bell for the last time.

Then I began the long trip to Illinois, and to Peter.

PROPHETS

Contra felicem vix deus vires habet

-Against a lucky man, a god scarcely has power

8

June 1, 2008
Unknown Location

I awoke from the attack with my head throbbing in an intense pain that was only slightly more prominent than the sharp crick in my neck. Opening my eyes to discover that a blurry shield of rough cloth had been placed over my face, I tried to pull it off, but my wrists had been tied to the arms of the chair where I was now seated. My legs were likewise restrained at the ankles. I turned my head as far as I could in both directions, sensing nothing.

"Anyone there?" No response. A moment passed, my breath hot and trapped to my face. I rolled my neck and flexed my back, feeling a sharp pain radiate outward from my spine.

Someone behind me said, "A .454 revolver seems like overkill for suicide, don't you think?"

This was not the voice from the hotel; it belonged to a different man, older, less intense, but more calculated.

"That's a matter of personal opinion, my friend. I hope you saved that fucking bottle."

"Why did you kill Peter McAlister?"

"Listen, I appreciate the friendly banter, but if you're going to blow my head off anyway let's just get on with it."

"You're on borrowed time already. I asked why you killed him."

"Tell me who you are and I'll tell you all about it. Or you could threaten to kill me and see how that works out."

"Why would I threaten to kill you?"

"The guy who put a gun in my mouth seemed pretty excited about the prospect."

"Of course he was. That's why he's the guy who puts guns in people's mouths. But I call the shots here."

"Why should I tell you? You're going to kill me, anyway."

"Killing you won't benefit either of us. There's something that matters more to you than living does, and if I like what you have to say I might offer it to you."

I snorted to clear a blocked nostril, swallowing as my mouth filled with mucus and the rusty taste of stale blood. "I don't care about money."

"You're an Afghanistan and Iraq vet who just graduated from West Point. You murdered a man and were about to kill yourself. I'll bet planning Peter's death has kept you going for weeks, and now that he's gone you've lost your last distraction from an almost overwhelming urge to commit suicide. I know you don't care about money, David."

"Decent thirty second psychoanalysis," I conceded.

"Now tell me why you killed Peter."

"Have you ever talked to him? I'm surprised no one shot him before I got around to it." I heard heavy footsteps begin pacing the room behind me, but when the voice spoke again, it remained stationary.

"As a matter of fact, I haven't."

"The man in the hotel said he was there when I killed Peter. Said he stood over the body before the brains had dried."

"He did. So did I."

"Where were you?"

"On your way out, you stopped for a second and listened, like you heard something in the trees alongside the house. You were looking right at us."

"Why were you there?"

"It's obvious, isn't it?"

"Apparently not, since I'm asking."

"We were there to kill Peter, too. And while I suspect our motives were singularly different from yours, I won't know until you tell me."

"Clearly, you've looked through my computer. Didn't that have everything you needed to know?"

"Almost. I know about your fiancée and your best friend, the medical condition that ended your military service, and the girl who left you when she read the contents of your laptop."

I released a long sigh and leaned my head back until my neck strained in protest. "Then I've either been knocked out for some time, or you're one hell of a fast reader."

"But I don't know why you came to Illinois, or why you chose Peter. That information wasn't documented in your writings. If no one paid you to do it, that leaves a personal motive, but after checking your background it appears you and he have never been in the same state at the same time, much less ever met, before today."

"What difference does it make?"

"To people like us, it's life or death."

"You know the girl who left me after going through my computer?"

"Yes."

"She left him for me. He didn't take it well."

"That's it?" he asked.

"That's it."

"But the best friend who slept with your fiancée is still alive."

"If he hadn't told me about the affair, I still wouldn't know. Now, can you take this bag off my head? Also, some water would be outstanding. Or, better yet, a glass of the bourbon that you better not have left in my fucking hotel room."

"I found the parachute in your truck and saw that you documented 150 BASE jumps—"

"154."

"—on your computer. Before I get your water, I'd like you to assess a particular building and tell me whether or not you could BASE jump off of it."

"Will it get the bag off my head?"

"Yes."

"Sold."

"Keep your eyes to the front."

The hood was ripped off my tender scalp and the onslaught of light shot daggers to the back of my skull. A headache blossomed in my brain as I inhaled only slightly less stale air—the room smelled like a cellar. A series of pages were taped on an unfinished stone wall in front of me. I started to turn my head sideways, but a figure standing behind me gently pushed my chin forward again.

"Eyes to the front. Look at the pictures."

The pages were printed at a high resolution and mostly contained satellite imagery of a city block at increasing levels of focus, narrowing in on a single building indicated by a small red arrow. Another series of photographs was taken from ground level at all angles around the base of the structure and included a park dotted with trees.

"It's thirty-eight stories," he said.

I studied the pictures for a minute, trying to blink the fog of pain from my mind. "Yeah, I can jump that."

"That's it?"

"I thought that's what you were looking for."

"Can you be more specific?"

"All right, I'd pack slider down with a vented forty-two inch pilot chute. Exit point would be the northwest corner of the roof. I'd take a two-second delay going handheld unless access to the exit point was technical enough to justify stowed. After opening, I'd cut a left turn to burn off altitude and then bring it back right toward the park, drive a flat turn between the trees, and sink it off into the grass."

"Why the northwest corner?"

"Best outs for off-heading openings. A ninety left would still allow me to pull a one-eighty and fly into the park. A ninety right would probably cause me to overshoot the landing area, but I could still make a one-eighty and touch down on that east to west-running street. And if I have a one-eighty on opening, a corner exit is my best chance to turn away before I strike the building."

"How difficult would this be?"

"Pretty fucking difficult. Worse if the winds don't cooperate, and in a city they never do."

"So you BASE jump, and you've got no family to answer to. Are you any good with a pistol?"

"I've been shooting pistols since I was eight, and you can ask your thugs how close I came to getting the draw on them at the hotel."

"Then I want you to jump this building for me next week."

"Why would you want me to do that?" The pacing footsteps behind me ceased.

"Because I want you to kill a man inside."

My mind ground to a halt. "Why the fuck would I kill someone for you, and what does that have to do with a jump?"

"Let's start with the second question. Once you get inside that particular building, the only way to go is up and the only way out is the roof."

"Then get him somewhere else," I said.

"If I could get him anywhere else, he'd already be dead."

"Who is he?"

"I cannot tell you that. I can train you and equip you, and I can get you inside with the knowledge of exactly where to find him. The rest is up to you."

"How do I know you won't kill me once I'm done?" The loud footsteps resumed as a second man began pacing again.

"You don't, but that's beside the point. Agree to this, David, and you'll get what you've been waiting for your whole life: the perfect rush. You've flirted with death, but you've not yet married her. There are others like you. The hard part is finding them, but in this case we've found you."

"Who is 'we?'"

"The scope of this proposal alone should give you an indication of what we do. You can be a part of that, or you can be drugged again and wake up in that beater of yours back in the hotel parking lot."

"I think you'd kill me if I refused. Acceptance under punishment of demise isn't really acceptance, is it?"

"Religions do it all the time."

"I don't go to church."

"Then what is your antenna across the river from West Point? You've been going to church. You just call it Ma Bell."

I couldn't parry his response. "This all seems like a ludicrous plan. No offense."

"Less imaginative than suicide in a hotel room with a bottle of scotch?"

"Bourbon."

"My point stands."

My legs began to fall asleep, so I tried shifting my weight in the chair. "What would this entire arrangement consist of?"

"You'd be more or less living under armed guard in a remote area. There will be no contact with the outside world. The next five days consist of shooting drills with a personal instructor, firing hundreds of rounds a day. When you're not shooting or loading magazines, you'll be memorizing the floor plans and schedules relevant to the target. On the sixth day, we get you into the building. You go to a designated place at a designated time, positively identify an individual, and kill him. Then you move to the roof, parachute off, and link up with our car. We get you off the site."

"Then what?"

"The book answer is that we pay you and then go our separate ways. But I've seen what you've written, and after this is done you'll be begging me for more work. Whether I hire you again depends on how well you perform this job."

"I told you why I killed Peter. I want to know why you were going to."

A few seconds passed before he said, "If you pull this off successfully, I'll tell you."

I tilted my head, scanning the pictures in front of me. "Then I'm in."

I heard the click of a pocketknife blade being flipped open. He cut my ankles free, and then sliced the restraints off my wrists.

"Let's go to work, David," he said.

I eased myself to my feet, my joints popping in protest, and stood before the photos of the building.

Then I turned to find three men standing behind me.

9

Alone in the darkness, I looked back on my life.

I didn't want to calculate the collective years spent with friends I would rather not have met, nor with the worthwhile ones who had either betrayed me or died along the way. Nor could I begin to gauge how much alcohol I'd drunk to continue drifting along in life, pursuing a meaningless degree that ended up being for naught.

Single, friendless, without family, I had trudged along toward an increasingly certain fate that I had spent decades building until my mind was trapped in its own confines beyond the point of no return.

After all that, what did I have to show for it?

I thought back to the moment I had stepped off the steel ramp of the helicopter during my first desert raid in Afghanistan, then to descending through the black sky under my parachute as I prepared to land in Iraq. Those few, precious bursts of electric intensity had repaid the many years that produced nothing worth remembering. The visuals associated with those moments—my palms sweating at the memories, the gunfights and combat and death—remained forever etched in my psyche.

And that, at its core, was the underlying issue beneath my endless pain. Beyond those collective moments, I spent my time feverishly, compulsively scratching at the surface of life, trying to recapture that feeling through every possible self-destructive tendency, only to fail at every turn.

BASE, by far, had come the closest—not many life issues could haunt you in the eerie twilight of life and death, where the most fleeting lapse in judgment or an unexpected gust of wind could transform you into a paralytic or a corpse before you had time to blink.

But, in the end, closing the distance toward humans intent on killing you as you tried to do the same to them was rivaled by no other adversary —not nature, not fate. There was no coming to grips with your own humanity quite like facing an opponent, guns in hand, knowing full well that only one of you would walk away.

I shifted in position, feeling my body settle on the foam beneath me. As I turned on a penlight, my gloved hands glowed with white light that stung my eyes. Squinting, I waited for my pupils to adjust within the confined space, my breath trapped around me.

Matz had painstakingly trimmed the sections of foam until they perfectly accommodated my body and my parachute, and then he fitted them to the interior of the five-foot metal cube. The box was identical to the shipping crates that passed through the underground loading dock in my target's building and was marked by a painted numerical identifier and a shipping label. The replica was complete with scuffs and dents, and had been surreptitiously fitted with ventilation channels on all sides.

Time should have slowed inside its tight confines, but it didn't. Instead, I found myself pleasantly surprised with each check of my watch as it ticked down toward zero, toward proving myself, toward an opportunity to return to combat. The parachute strapped to my back just made the anticipation that much more thrilling, and in the box I found myself more often than not filled with a sense of eagerness and focused on delivering a flawless performance, no matter the cost. Combat was on the line—it was a different kind than what I had experienced in war, to be sure, and also criminal in nature.

But it was combat.

What did I have to lose? Only a life I didn't care about. The possibility of death meant nothing to me; the prospect of combat, everything.

My watch ticked over to zero.

I carefully lifted the lid with my left forearm and leveled my Glock's suppressor as sunlight flooded the interior of the box.

Two images appeared in front of me—one of a cop pointing a handgun, the other of a blonde woman holding up her hands.

I fired two subsonic rounds into each picture, the *twirp twirp, twirp twirp* of the pistol splitting the foam-enclosed silence of the past hour. Spinning backward, I saw a staggering zombie with a bloody mouth, lit by sunshine and standing in scrub grass, and delivered two more shots to the center of its chest.

I reloaded before guiding the Glock suppressor through the cutout of my belt holster. A rolling breeze hit my face, cooling my sweat as I hoisted myself over the lid of the box and jumped down before sliding the top panel back into place.

Drawing my pistol as I whirled around, I scanned the forest. A long strip of white engineer tape stretched bumpily across overgrown grass and snaked into the trees. I heard the vague chanting of birds among the rustling treetops, their songs undisturbed despite my suppressed shots.

Transmitting into a mic dangling from my earpiece, I said, "Red, I send Kickoff. One crow and two parrots dead."

"*Copy Kickoff, one crow and two parrots,*" Boss responded through the receiver.

I trotted past the cop and the blonde woman, whose life-sized paper forms stretched across cardboard backings held up by long wooden stakes. Stopping before a piece of white engineer tape laid on the ground in the shape of a square, I pulled a color-coded key from a lanyard on my belt and pretended to insert it at waist level.

Matz called out from behind a tree, "What are you doing?"

"Activating the service elevator with the red key," I called back. "Pushing the top button for the fifteenth floor. Turning right, walking thirty feet to the stairwell."

Stepping out of the square, I turned right and walked toward another section of white tape, then stepped inside before transmitting, "Red, I send First Down."

"*Copy First Down,*" Boss transmitted.

I stepped inside the next square and called out to Matz, "Entering stairwell and walking to the thirty-second floor."

"Okay, you're there."

I transmitted, "Red, I send Second Down."

"Copy Second Down."

Taking a moment to focus, I began walking along the white engineer tape, mechanically calling out to Matz as I had already done dozens of times, "Left turn, twenty feet down the hall, right turn at the T-intersection, walk fifty feet and cross the office suite on my left, then to the secretary's office. Red, I send Third Down."

"Copy Third Down, stand by for confirmation."

Matz called out, "What's happening now?"

"Boss is calling the target's office phone to bring him to his desk. Secretary's door should be unlocked; otherwise, I open it with the white key."

"I have confirmation," Boss called through my earpiece. *"Execute. Execute. Execute."*

I keyed my radio twice to confirm before saying to Matz, "Boss cleared me. Now I cross the secretary's office to his door. If it's open, I enter; otherwise, I use the blue key. Walk inside and kill him."

There was no response. Glancing around the forest, the underbrush shaded beneath swaying treetops, I listened to the breeze and looked for tree trunks big enough to hide Matz's massive figure.

From somewhere to my left, he yelled, "Hit the range. Time starts now!"

I took a quick breath and turned, running fast down a worn trail into the woods that weaved past tree trunks and moss-covered rocks. Fifty feet into the trees, I heard Matz running behind me as he followed at a distance.

Bright sunshine lit the ground ahead as the trail gave way to a small clearing dotted with upright pieces of plywood barricades, beyond which the targets were arranged. I burst into the clearing and skidded to a halt behind the first barricade, drawing my Glock and using the wood as cover while I took aim at a chest-level rack topped with five steel plates.

I fired from left to right, missing the first plate but felling the other four in rapid succession before I hit the first plate with a sixth round. Conducting a magazine change behind cover, I walked laterally to my right, engaging four paper targets spaced out before the next barricade.

I fired three rounds before my pistol gave a hollow click.

Slapping upward on the magazine, I racked the slide to eject a bright orange dummy round and fired again within a second, continuing to walk and shoot as I thought about how pleased Matz would be with my speed.

I shot the fourth and final target twice before sprinting to the next piece of plywood and taking aim. Thirty feet beyond it was a Texas Star, a five-pointed wheel holding five steel plates in a wide circle. I shot the first plate, which dropped with a loud *clang*. The wheel began spinning, turning the remaining four plates into moving targets. Working my way clockwise, I shot them off the mounts without missing and took off at a sprint before the fifth had struck the ground.

A fifty-foot gap separated me from my final plywood barricade, and beyond it I could see the lone target representing my objective. He was a guardian angel, of sorts; without him, I would have been dead for days. As I closed with the firing position, breathing heavily and pumping my stiff limbs that strained after an hour spent hunched in the box, a succession of faces flashed through my head, an unsolicited procession of loss presented to me without warning— Sarah, Laila, and Peter before I shot him. Peter's face was replaced by the friend whose affair with Sarah ended my engagement, and he hovered in my mind for a fleeting second before Jackson appeared, smiling at me atop Ma Bell.

The last face I saw before arriving at the barricade was my own—a lopsided grin parting to insert a gun barrel.

I stopped behind the plywood, aligning my sights on a cardboard silhouette marked with the word *SAAMIR*. After firing one round that bored a neat hole between the *A* and *M*, the slide of my pistol locked to the rear.

Dropping the empty magazine, I reloaded a fresh one and straightened my arms in front of my body, then fired another two rounds into the letters and ran toward it, stopping a few feet away.

Assuming a wide firing stance, I raised my pistol.

A page-sized photograph was pasted over the head of the target showing a close-up of an olive-skinned man who looked younger than he was—the faint trace of a smile, dark eyes that gleamed from either side of a wide nose, immaculate black hair slicked back and neatly trimmed on the sides. He was wearing a suit with a violet tie and coordinated pocket square.

I fired five times into the photo, the .40 caliber rounds shredding a tight asymmetric pattern in the center.

Matz, forgotten in the trance of my routine, called out behind me, "Time stopped."

Without looking, I transmitted, "Red, I send Touchdown."

"*Copy Touchdown.*"

Then I holstered the Glock and turned around to find Matz watching me with a look of barely suppressed intensity and holding an M4 assault rifle that looked like a toy across his chest.

His perpetually dark-circled eyes looked unimpressed as I said, "Back to the hallway, turn right, fifty feet to a left turn, and twenty feet back to the stairwell."

I took a step inside another tape square and stopped with one foot in the air. Withdrawing a black mask from my pocket, I hastily pulled it over my head and adjusted the single oblong hole over my eyes.

Matz said, "If you forgot again, I was going to smoke you until the sun went down."

I cleared my throat before continuing, "Move up the stairs to the emergency exit at the top, where I walk in front of the only surveillance camera I can't bypass on my route. Fire alarm goes off when I open the door. Red, I send Extra Point."

"*Copy Extra Point,*" Boss replied.

"Walk to the northwest corner of the roof." I stopped at another tape marking and stripped off the security vest to reveal my BASE parachute underneath. Folding the vest, I stuffed it into a cargo pocket before transmitting again.

"Red, I send Game Over. Ten seconds."

"*Copy Game Over.*"

"Visually confirm getaway car location and then jump. Two second delay, canopy opens, land in the park. Stash my canopy in the bag, move a hundred feet to the west, climb over the fence, and get in the car. Mission complete."

Matz said nothing at first, and I glanced over to see him readying his M4 in my direction. "Unload and show clear."

I turned away from him, drew my pistol and unloaded it, then held it out to the side without turning. He took it from me, and I looked to the sky as a flock of white clouds drifted low overhead, moving in unison like flat-bottomed icebergs in the wind.

Matz yelled, "CLEAR!"

I sighed and turned around as he placed my Glock into an open holster on his left hip. His right side held an identical one without a suppressor.

Stripping the mask from my face, I shoved it into a pocket and smoothed my hair as Boss emerged from the woods.

He also carried an M4 and a sidearm, and he walked toward us with the measured cadence of an older man. His bearing belied the subdued expression of sadness that he wore at all times, a face that I still had trouble matching to the resolute voice that first spoke to me when I was tied to the chair.

He unslung his backpack and withdrew a bottle of water without slowing his pace, tossing it in a wide arc toward us.

"Thanks, Boss," I said, scrambling to catch it.

He examined me with tired but focused eyes, as if he had already seen everything but still had a debt to repay before he could retire. Keeping one hand on the pistol grip of his M4, he laid the other palm across the upper receiver with an air of nonchalance. "Let's talk contingencies for Chicago," he said. "What if you hear me transmit Penalty?"

I lowered the water bottle and stood up straight. "I'm compromised. Security knows I'm in the building."

"Forfeit?" he asked.

"Mission aborted. I get to the roof and jump."

"What if I call Forfeit when you're outside Saamir's office waiting for my confirmation?"

"I still go to the roof and jump. No exceptions."

He nodded. "Good, David. Your radio calls are getting better, but that's the first thing you're going to forget when your adrenaline is pumping. We'll be monitoring the security radio frequency but unable to transmit on it, so it's critical that I know your location in the building. If you forget to call in at a checkpoint, it could be the difference between me giving you an order that saves your life or one that kills you."

"Understood, Boss. I won't forget to call in."

"Go ahead, Matz," he said with a sigh of finality. "We might be waiting on Ophie for a minute."

Matz ran a tongue over his top row of teeth. "Suicide, your first targets out of the box were grouped well—you were hitting within a plate-sized area on all three. Then you got to the steel rack. Know why you missed the first plate?"

I took a sip of water. "Because it wasn't regulation-sized?"

"You went from a sprint to cracking off that first round the instant you stopped. I know plenty of guys who could make that shot, but you're not one of them. Stop, take a breath, and engage. On the four paper targets, your shot placement was perfect, but your group was too tight. You hit within a silver dollar-sized area on three of them, which means you should have been shooting faster. You dropped four seconds off your best range run, but you've still got a ways to go and we've only got time for a few more full rehearsals before game day. So don't get complacent on me." He looked at Boss. "That's all I've got."

Boss turned around, brought both hands to his mouth, and yelled, "Ophie! You fall asleep out there?"

A shout came back over the breeze, "No, man, I'm coming." Several long seconds passed before he sauntered out of the wind-swayed woods—a single figure, tall and lean, carrying a SCAR-H rifle loaded with match grade 7.62 rounds. The rifle was topped with a long scope, which, along with his lateness to our rehearsal meetings, conveyed the unspoken reality that he kept his barrel trained on me from a distance every time I was on the range with a weapon.

He strolled to a stop behind Boss and unzipped the backpack, removing a bottle of water and downing it in a few gulps. Long wisps of straw-colored hair were plastered to his forehead behind dark sunglasses, and when he finished drinking and wiped his mouth with the back of his wrist, he drawled, "Fuck, it is hot out here."

Boss and Matz looked at him wordlessly, prompting Ophie to add, "Regular funeral parlor with you guys. David, you still upset that Matz was on top of you in a cheap hotel room?"

I shook my head. "I'm a little disturbed that he had an erection when he did it."

"Fuck you, Suicide," Matz said.

Ophie smirked. "Jesus, lighten up people. If murder ain't fun, we're doing it wrong."

Boss shook his head. "You have anything to add?"

Ophie put a hand on his hip, angled his head toward the sky, and let out a long sigh.

"Well, since you all start these little group therapy sessions before I complete my death march in from the jungle, I don't know what's already been said. David, you're looking pretty good from what I can see. Getting fluid, none of that robotic shit you used to pull when we started out here. That'll serve you well when you're in the building with no backup. As soon as you get to the roof, I'll be able to see you with my long gun. Once you call ten seconds out from your jump, I'm going to smoke anyone in your landing area who looks like they'll be upset when a masked motherfucker comes down under a parachute like an angel of death. So be ready to vault some bodies on your way out."

I watched my reflection in his sunglasses and wiped a bead of sweat off my nose with a gloved knuckle. "Adrenaline turns me into a goddamn Olympian. Between killing Saamir and the jump, I'll vault whatever I need to."

Ophie scratched the back of his head, then looked at Matz and Boss.

"I'll be honest, fellas," he said to them. "I think the kid's ready."

10

I pushed the lid above my head, then rose from the box and angled my pistol into a firing position.

Seeing only rows of shipping crates and shelves lining unfinished concrete walls, I pushed the lid wide open and stood, sweeping the loading dock with my pistol. On the opposite wall I saw the wide service elevator and two steel doors lit by uncovered fluorescent bulbs. A soft hiss of air escaped from the ceiling as I inhaled the scent of concrete and dust, my senses ablaze with the imminence of a near-death experience. I used to BASE jump to replace the thrill of combat.

Tonight, I would get both.

I holstered the pistol and jumped down from the box, then secured its lid before moving behind a forklift to send my first transmission.

"Red, I send Kickoff."

"*Copy Kickoff. Happy hunting.*"

I rolled my shoulders forward to stretch my back and shook my legs one at a time to restore much-needed circulation. After bouncing three times on the balls of my feet, I strode toward the service elevator as adrenaline began trickling into my bloodstream. Each step felt more weightless than the last.

Inserting the red key beside the button panel for the service elevator, I turned it and waited as the doors slid open to reveal a cold, metal-lined interior. I entered and pushed the button for the fifteenth floor, drumming the fingers of one hand against my leg and the others against my holster as I waited for the doors to close.

After a delay of several seconds, they slid shut and the elevator lurched to life, beginning its unhurried rise. My heart pounded with dread as the elevator began inching to a halt before stopping loudly at the third floor. The doors whirred open to reveal a trim man with a short white beard. He was dressed in a pair of pressed khakis and a blue service shirt, a wide black case hung from a strap over his shoulder, and a large phone blinked from a clip on his belt. One hand held an aluminum clipboard stacked with papers.

"Evening," I said, trying my best to look official and calm.

He eyed me with surprise, then stepped in and said, "Evening, friend. You new at the company?"

"I'm down from regional."

He pushed the button for the eleventh floor and gave my security vest a suspicious glance as the doors closed. "Regional... aw, hell, this mean we got another one of those drills coming up?"

I shrugged noncommittally. "Lot of work orders tonight?"

"Oh, the entire building's falling apart—just ask anyone who works here. They canned three people off my staff from budget cuts and supposedly can't afford overtime for the rest of us, then I service orders at the offices up top that are decorated like the goddamn Art Institute."

"Maybe we both got into the wrong line of work."

"You said it." He eyed the floor indicator as it clicked past ten and the elevator began to slow. "Well, this is my stop. Have a good night."

I drew the Glock and fired once into his head at near point blank range. A dense fan of blood slapped the far side of the elevator and his black case thudded on the metal floor as he fell.

I quickly tapped a button before the doors had a chance to open and changed magazines as the elevator began moving toward my destination once more.

"Red, I send one parrot in the service elevator." Looking around the floor, I found the spent bullet casing and put it into my pocket. I repeated the radio transmission, but received no response from Boss.

After what seemed like an eternity, the elevator halted at the fifteenth floor. I drew my Glock as the doors slid open, ready to kill anyone unfortunate enough to witness the crime scene in the elevator.

Instead, I was confronted by a dark hallway with unadorned gray walls and a line of closed doors.

Holstering my pistol, I hit the button for the loading dock before stepping outside and transmitting again.

"Red, I send one parrot in the service elevator."

"*Copy one parrot.*"

"Need cleanup when your guy comes for the box. I just sent the elevator back down."

"*Negative, it's too late. Continue mission.*"

"Fuck," I whispered to myself, breathing quickly as I hurried down the hall to the stairwell door and pulled it open.

"First Down."

"*Copy First Down.*"

The stairway was wide and vacuous, and each footfall echoed amid a lingering smell of fresh paint. I took the gunmetal blue stairs at a brisk pace, turning past pipes and valves that ran up the corners at each landing. Every other turn of the stairwell revealed a door with a slim window above the handle and a neat stencil number marking the floor.

I reached 32 and stood to the side of the door.

"Red, I send Second Down."

"*Copy Second Down.*"

I took two measured breaths and walked through the door, moving down a clean hallway with neat carpet and light-toned wood grain walls that were lit by a row of small circular ceiling lights.

It was not my first time seeing the setting. Boss had shown me a video of this floor, taken from a hidden camera mounted on someone walking down the hall. The video was taken during business hours, and other people frequently blocked the distorted wide-angle view as it progressed through most of the route I was now walking.

Boss's voice crackled over my earpiece, "*Penalty. Penalty. Penalty.*"

I broke into a run and transmitted, "Get confirmation, I'm coming in hot."

As I took the right turn in the hallway, emergency strobes began flashing from the walls. An automated voice sounding from speakers in the ceiling said, "*Emergency alert. Active shooter. Enter the nearest room and lock the door. This is not a test. Wait for the all-clear from building security. Emergency alert. Active shooter...*"

The straightaway toward the office suite unfolded in front of me, and I catapulted down it in a panicked sprint as Boss said, "*Security is coming to get him. Two minutes out.*"

I skidded to a stop and reached for the wall to my left, yanking down on a fire alarm. A low, howling whistle gave rise to a high pitch before the automated voice reset. "*Emergency alert. Fire. Evacuate immediately...*"

As I took off again down the hall, Boss said, "*Forfeit. Forfeit. Forfeit.*"

"Get me confirmation," I said breathlessly.

"*You don't have time. Forfeit.*"

"Fucking call him!" I cut left into the office suite and ran past the reception desk and lobby. Desks and workstations were lined up in neat rows, and I flew by the conference room on my way to the secretary's corner office as a nauseating wave of fear ballooned in my chest.

"Third Down."

"*Negative confirmation. Forfeit.*"

I ran to the secretary's door to find it locked, and began fumbling to insert the white key on my belt. Turning the handle and flinging it open, I drew my pistol and saw light emerging from beneath the closed door to his office.

His phone was ringing.

I approached the door and quietly unlocked the handle.

Bursting inside, I sidestepped right to clear the doorway, catching glimpses of the desk and paintings but seeing no one as I swept my Glock left toward the far wall.

A deafening gunshot rang out, followed by a burst of flame that erupted beside his desk. Plaster dust exploded from the wall next to my head as I jumped sideways, wildly swinging my pistol toward the muzzle flash. I fired blindly, emptying a third of the magazine before my mind could process what I was doing.

A woman began screaming hysterically.

Racing behind the desk with my Glock up, I saw Saamir's body settling on the ground. Five bloody holes were stitched in his side and chest, and a revolver rested on the fingers of one hand. Beside his body, a woman was crouched on her heels and wore only a business skirt and black lace bra. Her eyes were wild with fear, and her expression was frozen in horror.

I pointed the gun at her face. "Don't look at me."

She turned her face downward and pressed trembling hands over her eyes as I shifted my aim to Saamir, centering the front sight post on the back of his motionless head. I cracked off two more rounds, and a pile of blood-soaked flesh exploded against the floor. I turned and ran out of the office, reloading as my eyes registered a decanter and two glasses on the desk arranged behind an unfolded magazine page containing a neat pile of white powder.

As I left the office, the woman's screams and the ringing phone were replaced by the fire alarm. "*...immediately. Emergency alert. Fire...*" I caught a transmission from Boss in my ear.

"*—already on your floor. Forfeit. Forfeit—*"

Turning the corner out of the secretary's office, I almost ran into two security guards. A massive black man was in the lead, followed by a tall white guard. Both wore matching navy uniforms and had drawn automatic handguns, their elbows bent and the barrels pointed upward like an old spy movie. I gunned down both of them, emptying the magazine as fast as I could pull the trigger. Puffs of pink mist exploded between us, and I reloaded on the run, darting past them into the office suite.

Sprinting along the right side of the room, I heard Boss say, "*—five more inbound to office suite—*" and ducked behind a desk as more guards thundered in and ran toward the woman's distant screams.

I thought through my escape route as I waited for them to pass, recognizing that any wrong turn would be fatal. I stood and flew toward the door of the office suite before hooking a right into the hallway. I had only taken three or four running steps back in the direction I had come from when two more guards appeared around the corner from my stairwell. Slowing to a walk, I fired half a magazine at them. Both were caught by surprise and tried to scramble back around the corner, but one caught a bullet to the shoulder blade and tumbled to the ground as I emptied the rest of my magazine at him.

Then I turned and ran in the opposite direction of my escape route as gunshots erupted behind me.

I passed the door to the office suite and heard one of the guards yelling as shots cracked through the air. A flurry of bullet holes pockmarked against the far wall as I flung myself down the first turn in the hallway. I reloaded while running and desperately tried to recall the building layout. I cut left down a side hall, finding a long straightaway before the next turn but knowing they'd be upon me long before I reached it.

Turning quickly, I crouched down at the corner and faced back the way I'd come. Within seconds, the lead men from the security force appeared, and I opened fire. The first two guards overexposed themselves and fell in a hail of bullets. I took aim at the first guard in the hall who was now trying to crawl to safety on his elbows. I shot him in the head, then took aim at the second who was lying motionless beside him before firing again.

My pistol went empty.

I rose and took off running down the long hallway before the guard force composed itself to pursue. Reaching for a fresh magazine from my belt, I found none. I dug into my pocket, grabbed a partially-full magazine from earlier, and slammed it into the pistol with a euphoric feeling of relief that didn't quite override the pull of panic in my mind.

Rounding the next corner, I saw my last hope of salvation: an exit sign above a nearby door marking the sole alternate stairwell to the roof. I raced toward it in desperation, hearing gunshots behind me just as I flung myself through the door.

I began taking the steps three at a time. Amid the muted fire alarm and emergency alert, I soon heard the rushing footsteps of the guard force chasing me. I fired a few rounds behind me as I ran, hoping the bullets ricocheting off the walls below me would slow their advance. As I passed the thirty-sixth floor, my pistol went empty. I reloaded with my last partially-full magazine while bounding up the steps.

Boss transmitted, "*They think you're on the west stairwell. They're sending a team up the east stairs, trying to beat you to the roof. Front line trace thirty-seventh floor.*" I was just crossing the thirty-eighth floor when he added, "*They're already on the roof.*"

I leapt up the final stretch of stairs, holding my left arm over my unmasked face in a desperate attempt to conceal it from the surveillance camera as I shouldered my way through the rooftop door.

A stiff breeze of warm, fishy air hit me as I stumbled into the darkness, wheeling right to see two men advancing through shoulder-height air units that hummed loudly. I fired on both of them, but had no idea if my rounds found their targets as I transitioned to another man standing on the opposite side of the roof. Muzzle flashes sparked as various guards returned fire.

Shooting my final bullet, I felt the Glock's slide lock to the rear.

I turned and leaned forward into a hard sprint, letting the pistol fall out of my grip and bounce off the ground. As I ran, I unzipped the vest with both hands and writhed out of it, pulling my arms out and letting it go as I neared a waist-high cinderblock wall. I took a single running leap, planting one foot on top of the ledge and propelling myself forward as hard as I could.

I soared into the emptiness beyond.

Time slowed to a crawl as my body fell in a wide arc away from the building nearly four hundred feet above a line of cars. Their headlights formed a river that flowed through the base of buildings whose every surface glittered with the stars of a thousand lit windows. I tried to slow the flailing of my arms and legs to assume a stable freefall position as I coasted above two fire trucks spinning an eerie red glow that whirled reflections off the street below me.

The ground rush grew to a deafening roar and lights accelerated upward in a trembling trajectory as I struggled to bring my wheeling right hand behind my waist. I was falling low, too many seconds into a prolonged delay by the time I finally grasped my pilot chute and frantically threw it out to the side.

My body accelerated exponentially toward the pavement as I involuntarily braced for impact.

I was jerked upright by a loud *crack,* the echo drowned by sirens as I ripped my steering toggles free and pulled my left arm down below my waist. The steep, oscillating turn barely prevented me from flying into the building to my front, and I tried to reverse course to line up with the side street on my right. My body swung left like a pendulum.

I registered scattered pedestrians along the sidewalk next to illuminated storefronts twenty feet below me as I maneuvered the toggles to slow the canopy in its final seconds of flight. My left arm was locked straight down and my right was above my waist in an instinctive bid to achieve level flight, and against all instinct I held course until the asphalt rose to meet me. A near-sideways image of four teenagers laughing around a table through a restaurant window seared itself into my mind a millisecond before impact.

My feet were pitched far forward of my body as my left side slammed into the sidewalk so hard that my vision exploded in bright flashes of light.

I tried to gasp for air but couldn't, the wind knocked out of my lungs as I rolled to a stop and my canopy fell limply behind me. I felt like I was going to suffocate. Struggling to find the cutaway handle on my harness, I weakly pulled it a moment before unseen hands grabbed me under the arms and hoisted me to my feet. I vaguely heard a loud voice call out to me as I sucked down my first gasps of oxygen.

"Holy shit! You a fucking skydiver, bro?"

The wide face of a twenty-something man hovered in front of me, reeking of alcohol, and my blurry vision registered several others clustering around us.

"Taxi," I slurred.

He howled with laughter before he boomed, in a Great Lakes accent, "Bro, your diming is perfect—you just missed a shidload-a cops rolling 'dru here!"

I tried to muster a weak smile as I continued gasping for oxygen and was hit with the smell of fresh pizza and stale car exhaust. The men shuffled me into a nearby cab and helped me into the back seat.

"Drive," I said.

"Wait!" a voice called from the sidewalk. "Hold dat cab!" One of the young men ran up holding my cut-away parachute, which was now balled into a mess of lines and risers. He set it on my lap and slapped me on the shoulder.

"Be careful out der, man, dat shit looks crazy!"

"Yeah. Stick to tennis." I closed the car door.

"Where to?" the driver said.

"Pullman Industrial Park."

He pulled away at an unhurried pace, leaving me to inhale deep breaths in the back seat as I vaguely took in the clusters of people smoking cigarettes outside a row of bars.

As my head cleared from the impact, I finally began to feel the wash of endorphins that always followed a jump. I knew I had an hour at best before the adrenaline wore off and my body would feel like it had been struck by an eighteen-wheeler. In my mind, I saw the screaming woman's face and wondered what the team would say. I didn't know if I would be alive by sunrise—either they had always planned on killing me once the job was finished, or they would now for disregarding the order to abort. I could have chosen to run, but knew that, on my own, my odds were worse.

And, as Boss had predicted, I wanted more work.

Feeling around my neck for the earpiece that had dislodged when I hit the sidewalk, I placed it in my ear and spoke quietly into the mic.

"Red, I need immediate pickup at Go To Hell Point 2. Touchdown."

KARMA

In cauda venenum

-In the tail, poison

11

"Well, was she hot?" Ophie asked.

"Yeah," I said.

He shrugged his acceptance.

Matz yelled, "What difference does that make? Was she Asian?"

"No."

"Then she wasn't that fucking hot, now was she? Why didn't you shoot her, Suicide?"

"She was wearing lingerie, for Christ's sake."

"We give you pregnant women and zombies for training targets, and you choke when you see panties? What are you, thirteen?"

Like most meetings in the house, this one occurred while seated around the oak dining table set atop linoleum flooring that cracked at the edges. I gazed through the sliding glass door behind Boss toward the bleached wooden porch that gave way to the overgrown yard where I had spent hours in the crate. Past that, dense woods were split by a trail leading to the range where I had prepared for killing Saamir.

"In his defense," Ophie said, "he ended up needing the ammunition."

Boss turned his gaze to me. "Five magazines would have been plenty if he'd aborted when I told him to."

"If I had aborted, Saamir would still be alive."

Matz replied, "The next time you disobey Boss, you won't be."

Boss stopped him with a raised palm before turning to me. "David, this was not intended to be a high-profile event. Since you didn't abort when ordered, we've got a trail of bodies that has created a media spectacle. We took care of the taxi driver, but there are still the pedestrians who saw your face—for all we know, they could be working with police sketch artists in Chicago as we speak. And let's not forget that anyone on the street would have just as likely detained you as helped you into a taxi, especially if you had a gun, which you would've had if you didn't leave your fucking pistol on the objective."

"I think he learned his lesson, guys," Ophie said. "Poor bastard was on the run from the Mongolian horde and took a swan dive off the top of a building for his efforts. I couldn't smoke guys on the roof fast enough, and David didn't even notice. If he had fumbled with his vest or tripped on his way to the edge, he'd be in the morgue right now instead of back here with us. He's got combat under his belt, and he's cut his teeth a bit on our side where the lines blur. I say we take him."

"He only did two trips," Matz said. "Then he bailed from Regiment and spent the last five years in a classroom, trying to be a fucking officer. No offense, Boss."

Ophie countered, "But he probably killed as many people last night as I did on my second deployment."

"If there were a way out of that building other than the roof, it would have been me in there. His parachute routine is a one-trick act."

Boss said, "It's a skill set. But this isn't the line of work for someone who second-guesses orders."

"I fucked up, Boss," I said. "It won't happen again."

He looked at me. "You understand what employment on this team would mean."

"I understand."

"If your enemies don't kill you in this business, your employers might."

"Understood."

"And if you follow this path any further, you'll ultimately have to leave the country. And it's a hard, dangerous road to even earn that. Or, you can take your money from killing Saamir and leave now."

"I won't make it on my own."

Matz said to Boss, "We're not a depression rehab center. And being down a man shouldn't be an excuse to keep everyone we bring in for a job. We're not getting Caspian back."

Boss looked at me. "David, leave us."

I looked at their faces, then placed my hands on the table to brace myself as I stood, pain rippling through me. As I left the dining room, I heard Ophie say, "The kid's been a sponge for the past week. Imagine where he could be if we work with him..."

The interior of the remote house struck me as a place where Daniel Boone would have come to smoke pot. I walked stiffly over the scarred wooden floor of the living room, passing between battered couches and recliners that were surrounded by bookshelves stacked with dust-covered titles. Walking through an open doorway, I eased my body down the narrow staircase leading to two closed doors.

The room on the left led to the cellar where Boss had first interrogated me. I turned right and opened the opposite door.

My room was sparsely furnished with cheap wooden furniture, its walls painted long ago in an oppressive shade of mustard yellow. Dresser drawers were filled with nondescript articles of men's clothing that didn't belong to me but likely shared the same original owner as the running shoes I had found under the bed.

I lowered myself onto the edge of the mattress, and the springs creaked loudly. My entire body ached from crash landing onto the sidewalk, with the worst soreness reserved for my left side. Lying on my back, I rested my hands at my sides and tried to straighten my spine. Sooty cobwebs clung to the corners of the graying ceiling, and above that I could hear the indistinguishable murmur of voices in the kitchen.

I closed my eyes.

Should I have shot the woman? In truth, the thought hadn't even occurred to me—I told her not to look at me, and she didn't. I performed my job and left. If one of us had to die, it was better me than her.

Releasing a long, slow exhale, I rubbed my throbbing left shoulder and brushed aside the thought.

Flashing images of the previous night ticked through my mind. I didn't want to stop after only one job. The prospect of additional missions was a lifeline I wanted to cling to against the currents threatening to sweep me away. I thought back to my meeting with the colonel after finding out I was non-commissionable: *Telecomm and corporate sales are pretty hot right now.* I thought about an alternate future—Laila trying to check up on her platonic charity case of an ex, guilt-ridden that she couldn't deal with my disease when she'd had the chance. Why would she? Why did she ever even get in bed with me: a fucked up foster kid with a failed engagement and a head full of memories from a war that nobody cared about anymore?

But racing through that building and shooting at armed men in a desperate plea to make it to the roof—it was a waking dream, a life-altering event that made use of all my fucked up experiences. I didn't care how bad my body hurt today. I didn't care that the girl was left alive. And, throughout the planning and execution of that mission, I certainly didn't care about Sarah or Laila or anyone else.

I didn't care about the Army, either—four wasted years at West Point, five counting the prep school, and I wasn't good enough to serve in combat again? Now, I had done something far more dangerous than I ever had in war, something that command would never have approved in the first place. And if it had happened, they would have been pinning medals on my chest.

Fuck the Army, I thought, and fuck Boss and Matz. If they wanted to kill me over how I dealt with Saamir, they could go right ahead. If they banished me, I'd just finish the fucking job I started the night I met them. I couldn't force their hand in giving me more work any more than I could force the Army's hand into letting me serve, so they could take me as I was. Either that, or I'd have one last night of writing and drinking and let my laptop tell the parts of my story that could be told. If it ended up in a land-fill unread, what the fuck did I care?

Matz yelled from upstairs, interrupting my thoughts.

"David! Get your fucking ass up here!"

I opened my eyes and checked my watch, seeing that half an hour had passed. Grunting as I rolled over, I stood and ascended the narrow staircase to the team.

"Have a seat," Boss said as I entered the dining room. I did so, trying to conceal my pain and observing that none of them had moved from their chairs.

He raised a hand to rub his temple. "Mistakes are going to happen, David. I accept that. I'm not going to fault you for leaving that girl alive after she'd seen you. I would argue that you went into a complex situation with minimal training because we were on a timeline. Nobody expected this to be a flawless incursion. But I cannot tolerate you, or anyone else, blatantly disregarding an order. You made it out last night because of blind luck and because the guards probably only shoot their weapons twice a year."

I nodded deferentially. "You're right, Boss."

"Regardless of your lack of judgment in disregarding an order, your military experience is insubstantial given what we do. You just don't have the background we're looking for and, given your medical condition, you never will. However"—he lowered his hand and set it flat on the table between us—"we are down a man and things are about to get busy. We can't accept you as an equal partner, but we can give you a chance as a trainee. Under any other circumstances, you wouldn't be a candidate at all. Your continued employment will be on a daily basis. If we don't like something we see out of you again, you're gone."

Matz leaned forward and rested his elbows on the table, his massive hands forming a cupped fist under his chin. "The odds are stacked against us enough as it is. Don't make it worse by doing something dumb, like ignoring an order when Boss is trying to get you out alive. And if you endanger the life of anyone here, least of all me, I'll kill you in a fucking second and not think twice about it. Got it?"

"I got it, Matz."

Ophie was leaning back in his chair and didn't move an inch as he said, with his eyes on mine, "I guess I'm in the minority here. I saw you on the roof, brother. And I'd fight beside you any day. Not saying you're God's gift to the death squad, but no one who did this job ever felt prepared for it. Most of them had a lot more experience than you. So don't be too hard on yourself. Next time, shoot the bitch and come home when Boss rings the dinner bell."

Before I could speak, Matz said, "All right, Suicide, the vacation's over. Our next job is coming up, and depending on what the target individual does we'll either be hitting a convoy or a house. I hope you remember how to use an M4, because we need to get you proficient with long shots and room clearing. And the security detail won't be unionized this time. They're professionals who have no issues killing cops, much less other criminals. So stop limping around and feeling sorry for yourself. Your training resumes today."

12

He was naked when I entered the cellar, save for a hood over his head.

The chair looked unsuited to the task of supporting his massive frame, and the restraints that bound him seemed insubstantial against his sweat-soaked muscles. Neat lines of Cyrillic script covered his left rib, while the opposite shoulder bore a mottled burn scar that extended halfway down his chest, which rose and fell with each shallow breath.

Instead of facing the wall that used to hold pictures of Saamir's building, the chair was now facing black supply boxes. Matz sat on top of them, staring at the man without emotion, and Boss stood beside him drinking coffee. I quickly took a seat next to Matz.

Ophie entered the room with a casual gait, walking across an overlaying carpet of blue tarps covering the floor. Approaching a rickety foldout table several feet from the man in the chair, he let his hand drift over a selection of tools—a power drill, pruning shears, a knife, a hammer, a hacksaw—before selecting a thin syringe. He picked it up and held it to the light, pointing the needle upward and delicately flicking the tube.

He approached the chair and roughly injected the solution into the unconscious man's arm. We watched the bowed and hooded head, waiting. Within seconds, his shallow breathing quickened, culminating in a sudden gasp. He lifted his head, and the hood swung from one side to the other as we waited in silence.

"I'm awake," the man said with a low, Eastern European accent.

Ophie ripped off the hood, and the man squinted and blinked while appraising his surroundings. He was bald and unshaven, with deep-set eyes that flashed from Ophie to Boss and Matz before finally settling on me.

"Refilling the ranks quickly, I see. Who's the kid?"

Ophie said, "Luka, David. David, this is Luka."

The man's eyes didn't move from mine. "I don't know you."

Ophie snapped his fingers, directing Luka's attention back to him. "What do you have, stage fright? Mind your fucking business."

Luka stared at Ophie in defiance. "I'm not going to tell you anything."

"*Iyam nut guing to tale zchou anyzching?* That's adorable. All this time in America and you still sound like a fucking movie villain. And relax, this isn't an interrogation."

"Then what is it?"

"Adjudication. We know you killed Caspian. You're just here to answer for it. And now that we've got that out of the way, you can say anything you want from now until I actually kill you, which won't happen for the longest hour or so of your fucking life. You can sing the Macedonian National Anthem, for all I care. But if I were a gambling man, I'd bet you're just going to scream a whole lot."

"If it makes you feel better, go ahead and kill me. I'm ready."

"Oh, it will definitely make me feel better. But you know what else will? When we find your manager and do some interior decorating with his brain matter."

"Good luck finding him. I don't even know his location, and torture is not going to change that."

"I believe you, Luka. He's pretty good on the run. If he could go back to high-society living or just lower his goddamn standards back to the underground, we'd find him. But bouncing around white suburbia rental properties? That's a stroke of genius. Ian's been having a hell of a time trying to locate him for us."

"Too bad."

"Funny thing is, Saudis have that stubborn sense of personal honor. I bet if his nephew were killed, he'd come pay his respects to the grieving father. What do you think?"

"You'll never get to Saamir, either."

"Really? That's interesting, because Saamir is dead."

Luka watched Ophie for a moment. "That's bullshit," he said flatly.

"No, he's fucking dead, along with seven guys from the security detail. Ian's been running surveillance on his father since before the trigger got pulled, and with the funeral coming up, I'd say it's just a matter of time before your boss comes slithering in at some godforsaken hour of the night. You know what happens after that."

"If you could have gotten to Saamir, you would have killed him before now."

"Sorry you've missed out on current events during your fourteen-hour ride in a trunk, but he's dead as a stump. Seems someone lit him up in his office while he had a coke spoon in one hand and his CFO's tit in the other."

"You couldn't even get into his building."

"Getting in wasn't the problem, Luka. Problem was getting out. Guess who pulled that off?"

Luka's stare, intensified with rage, fixed on Matz.

Ophie followed Luka's eyes. "Not this time, Luka. Matz just drove the getaway car. Saamir got his head blown off by the new guy. Turns out he likes to jump off skyscrapers and shit. Don't believe me?"

Luka looked me up and down. "No. I don't."

"I'll make you a bet. If Saamir is alive, I'll let you walk out of here right now. Hell, I'll drive you to the nearest bus station and send you on your way with a ham sandwich. But if you're wrong" —Ophie rocked his head back and forth as if considering his options—"I get to torture and kill you, then put your corpse in the freezer like you did with my best friend's body for four days before you dumped him—"

Matz interrupted, "There's no room in the spare freezer. I made a grocery run a few days ago. You know there's no room."

"Then throw out some fucking chicken breasts. You cook them every night, and I think I speak for everyone here when I say we'd prefer anything else at this point. And we all know you're too much of a spineless pussy to touch Boss's ice cream."

"The ice cream stays," Boss said with a grim sense of finality, leaning over to look at Matz. "That's not up for debate."

Matz said, "It's a two-hour drive to the store, Ophie. Two. Hours."

Ophie released a frustrated sigh. "Fine, goddammit. Luka, I'll cut your head off, put *that* in the freezer, if I'm lying about—"

"ENOUGH!" Luka yelled. "I don't fucking believe you!"

Ophie spun in place, pulling his phone from his pocket and thrusting the screen toward Luka. "Read 'em and weep, you Macedonian piece of shit!"

Luka's face twisted into a mask of hatred. "I'll kill you. *I'LL FUCKING KILL YOU ALL!*"

Ophie leaned down, placed a hand on Luka's straining shoulders, and said, "Easy, easy now. I forgot you two used to be close. Luka, your friend Saamir is in a better place now. God has a plan, and sometimes that plan involves half a dozen Hydra-Shok hollow points and total destruction of the central nervous system."

Luka composed himself, but his breathing came in quick bursts through flared nostrils. "My employer's men will kill you long before you get to him."

"Well aren't you just the most optimistic guy to ever be tied to a chair." Ophie turned to us, putting on a pair of shooting glasses from his shirt pocket. "Gentlemen, go ahead and don some eye protection."

Boss retrieved three sets of identical plastic glasses from a box beside him and handed two of them to Matz. I looked at Matz questioningly when he offered me a pair.

Matz asked, "Do you know how far or in what direction bone chips will fly when you push a drill bit straight through a human kneecap?"

"No."

"Neither do we."

I put on the glasses.

Ophie lifted a power drill from the table and pulled the trigger. The long bit whirred to life, the sound resonating off the cellar's stone walls before falling silent. I began to feel sick to my stomach.

Luka hyperventilated, his upper body starting to spasm and bead with sweat, but his eyes stared resolutely forward.

Ophie knelt and pulled the trigger again, pressing the spinning metal bit into Luka's left knee. The drill's high whine suddenly reduced to a sickening dull tone.

Luka bucked wildly in the chair and screamed so loud it made me jump. Ophie studied the end of the bloody drill bit emerging from the opposite side of the leg, and then pulled it back out.

"IT WASN'T ME! IT WAS THE IRANIAN!" Tears and saliva ran down Luka's face, pouring over the sweat in a race to his throat.

I shifted in my seat and whispered to Matz, "Who is the Iranian?"

"He's dead already. Stop talking."

Ophie set the drill back on the table, exchanging it for a hammer. Next, he selected the pruning shears; after that, a hacksaw. Luka's voice went hoarse from screaming as the stale, musty cellar air filled with a metallic-septic odor that grew in intensity with each passing minute.

I felt nauseous and began wondering if Boss was going to tell Ophie to kill Luka instead of drawing out the process any longer. Glancing over, I watched Boss flinch as flecks of blood flew onto the side of his coffee mug. He looked momentarily irritated as he examined the surface of his coffee to make sure his drink was unscathed, and then took another sip. Feeling Matz's eyes upon me, I turned my head toward Luka, watching the scene though I didn't want to.

Throughout the process, Ophie never rushed.

He remained patient, speaking quietly to Luka as he worked with the practiced efficiency of a hunter field dressing a trophy buck. When the chair fell over from Luka's violent resistance, Ophie set it back upright and resumed what he was doing. As the dying man took his last breaths, Ophie retrieved a knife with a broad, dark gray blade that extended seven inches to a tapered point.

"Say hello to Caspian for us," Ophie said before slicing Luka's throat with wide, consistent strokes, sawing back and forth until he'd reached the vertebrae. He shortened his strokes and quickened the pace until Luka's head separated from his body. The head fell to the ground and rolled onto its side, until two bloody eye sockets faced us in a hollow stare.

My blood ran cold, and I looked over to see Matz appraising my face. "You'd better toughen up before you get someone killed," he said. "Meet me on the range with your long gun and full kit, ready to go, in half an hour. And puke before you show up."

He rose and left the cellar.

Boss took a step toward me and touched my shoulder. "Welcome to the war."

Then he walked out behind Matz.

Ophie still held the knife, and every surface from the tip of its blade to halfway up his forearm was masked by dark, arterial blood. He stood over Luka's remains, breathing slowly and methodically, and by all appearances was completely unaware of my presence in the room.

13

"Just pull through the gate onto the tarmac," Boss said. "There he is."

Our headlights found the opening in a low chain link fence and Matz steered the truck through it. A distant figure guided us with the wave of a flashlight, its beam pirouetting on the ground beside the long profile of a single-engine plane. Moonlight gleamed off its smooth metal surfaces, and as we got closer I recognized familiar lines forming a Cessna Caravan, an aircraft I had skydived from hundreds of times. Matz stopped just short of the tail as the man extinguished the flashlight, and we exited the vehicle under an ink-black sky sprinkled with stars.

The man standing beside the plane was easily in his sixties, with trim silver hair topping a gaunt face between jug ears. One hand tucked a small flashlight into the pocket of his flight jacket; the other held an enormous green thermos.

"Joe," Boss announced, stepping forward to shake his hand. "Great to see you."

Looking around at the rest of us, the man replied in a husky voice, "Likewise, Boss. Special K isn't coming on this one?"

"Waiting for us at the destination."

"Leave anyone behind?"

"No. We're down to four now."

He nodded. "Sorry to hear that. What's your total weight with men and equipment?"

"Just under fourteen hundred pounds."

Joe whistled. "More than usual."

Matz said, "Ammunition is heavy. We'll be lighter on the way back."

"No doubt in my mind. You boys can go ahead and load up while I finish my pre-flight, and we can take off in about twenty minutes. We'll be in the air for three and a half hours, refuel and take a piss break, and then have another two-hour hop. Plenty of time for you to catch some sleep and get ready for the big game."

As we began transferring cases from the truck to the plane, I asked no one in particular, "What is Special K?"

"A fucking pain in the ass," Matz replied. He slid a black supply box off the back of the truck and carried it in front of him with both arms.

"That has wheels, you know," Ophie called after him.

"Fuck you."

I said to Ophie, "So Matz is angrier than usual. Perfect."

"Half of everything he says is just playing bad cop to make sure you take shit seriously."

"And the other half?"

"He's a dick." Ophie grabbed a rifle case with each hand and followed Matz. I hoisted two kit bags behind my shoulders and walked through the darkness toward the aircraft.

Boss rolled a box beside me, looked me up and down, and said, "You seem nervous."

"Let's go with confused. What is Special K?"

"You'll find out soon enough. I don't think you, of all people, will be disappointed."

"Who is Ian, then?" We stopped in front of the cargo door to help each other load the bags and boxes.

"When former direct action guys go freelance, you get us. We're an action arm. When former intelligence guys go freelance, you get a group like the one Ian is part of."

"So he's not the leader?"

Boss started walking back to the truck. "No. Ian is just our account manager. There might be ten guys working around the clock when we commission work from him, but Ian is the only face we'll ever see."

"Why?"

"To keep them isolated. We liaise directly with our employer, which comes with its own set of risks."

"Who is our employer?"

Boss hoisted one kit bag from the truck, then another. He turned to me and paused for a moment before saying, "Someone I hope you never get to meet."

"Who is he?"

"We call him the Handler. Get some bags." He turned and walked back to the plane. I grabbed a carry-on bag with each hand and rushed to follow him. Matz knocked into my shoulder as he passed.

"You said if I pulled off the last job you'd tell me why you were going to kill Peter."

Boss asked, "What do you know about him?"

"Laila said he was in grad school."

"That's probably what he told her. He was a delivery driver, and he used to move packages to Saamir's building."

"So?"

"When we asked for a way into the building, Ian had one of his guys befriend Peter and elicit information. That eventually allowed Ian's guys to get a box into the loading dock with you in it, and get it back out once it was empty."

"You were going to kill him because he saw the face of one of the guys from Ian's group?" We hoisted the bags onto the plane.

"Employees are high on the suspect list when something sensitive gets leaked. He could have talked."

"The pilot could talk. You're not going to kill him, are you?"

Boss stopped. "Joe is a living legend. Thirty-five years of service before he went private sector, and he's seen more trouble than the rest of us combined. Remember that when you get a few jobs under your belt and start to think you're tough. Now load the fucking plane."

* * *

Ophie strode into the hotel room, pushed aside Boss's luggage, and lay on the mattress. Folding his hands behind his head with a contented sigh, he closed his eyes.

"Make yourself at home," Boss said, closing the door behind Matz.

I took a seat on the foot of the bed, noting without surprise that the room shared the same drab arrangement of hideous wall art and patterned carpet as the room I'd just checked into. Boss pulled the curtains shut, blocking out the view of the parking lot before settling himself into a chair. He put on his reading glasses and began appraising an open newspaper on the desk.

Matz cracked his knuckles and asked, "Where is he?"

Without looking up from his newspaper, Boss answered, "Should be here any minute."

Shaking his head, Matz began pacing between the window and the door like a caged animal. Ophie appeared to be asleep beside me. I heard a soft knock at the door, and Matz lunged forward and flung it open. A balding, wiry man wearing khakis, a plaid shirt, and a leather satchel slung over his shoulder entered the room.

"What took you so long?" Matz asked.

Boss walked past me and greeted the man with a handshake and a hug. "Ian, this is our new hire, David."

Ian's face creased into a wide smile, and he took my hand and pulled me into a half-hug. "Pleasure to meet you, brother. Nice work on Saamir, by the way. Hopefully the button cam footage helped—one of our guys spent half a day in a suit for that."

"Absolutely," I said. "The hallways looked very familiar as I sprinted down them with bullets flying past my head."

Ian looked behind me and saw Ophie on the bed. "Nice to see you, too. No need to get up."

Ophie's eyes remained closed as he replied, "We're exhausted, Ian. I'll only be able to muscle down six or seven beers before I pass out. Better get this briefing over with quick."

Ian set his satchel on the bed and removed a stack of papers, then began arranging them on the red floral comforter. Ophie reluctantly sat up.

Pointing to a picture of a round-faced Middle Eastern man with a neatly trimmed moustache, Ian said, "We got positive identification on the target last night when he visited the grieving father. In order to extrapolate where his route would take him and his entourage in the coming days, we had to obtain the identity of the personal assistant and run his finances, which took my staff no small amount of effort. Short story is that one of the bank accounts he accesses routinely has been used to pay for rental properties in several states. Since their safe house network isn't .as extensive this far south, we looked for new activity and found that they're paying rent at six new houses across three states. Once we determined the houses they stayed at on the route to Saamir's father, we were able to refine the most likely—"

"Ian," Boss said, "it's late. We're tired. What's the target?"

Ian sighed and rubbed his earlobe between his thumb and forefinger. He pushed aside the photograph to reveal the stack of pages. "Bottom line, this is the house where you want to hit him. It's about a forty-minute drive from here, and he'll be arriving tomorrow afternoon and leaving the following morning. That gives you roughly a sixteen-hour window to action the target. The property itself is at the end of a cul-de-sac, so you can do a vehicle drop-off two kilometers away and move sight unseen through the woods right up to the back door. Down the street is another house that's being remodeled, so there aren't any tenants and the work crews don't arrive until ten in the morning. You can put Ophie there with his sniper rifle when it's dark and he'll have full coverage over the front of the target house."

Ophie asked, "What's the range on that?"

"Four hundred meters," Ian replied, pointing to a page with overhead imagery of the neighborhood and surrounding area. "And here are the floor plans."

Matz snatched the pages from Ian and flipped through them. "Second floor is going to be tricky. How many people?"

"Four security guys and two principals. They're moving in a Sprinter van that can pass for a service vehicle from the outside, but it's been modified into a mobile office. Our primary and his personal assistant work in the back, and up front they've got one security guy driving and three riding."

"What kind of hardware are they running?"

"At this point, we haven't seen any weapons carried openly. Best guess is

AR platforms, if not MPs or UMPs—something like that. Plus pistols. Nothing you guys haven't seen before. And there's another factor we have to consider: that Sprinter van has been used as a mobile office since your target has been on the run. If I can get into it while you're clearing the house, I can pack up their hard drives for data recovery. The information we pull from those could feasibly end up being a bigger blow to their organization than killing the primary. I'd drive the goddamn thing off the objective if the cops wouldn't roll me up on the way out."

Boss responded, "Matz is the assault leader. It's up to him."

Matz looked at the floor plan. "Once we hit the staircase, you could enter through the backside and move to the garage. But you'd be on your own—I'm not stopping to clear the garage, because my priority is isolating the second floor."

"I can take care of myself," Ian said. I saw Ophie smirk as Ian continued, "Just be aware that these guys are willing to sit and fight it out. If they can't escape, they'll strongpoint the primary and make you fight for every inch of that house until the cops arrive."

Matz's eyes danced over the pages, his nostrils flaring as he breathed. "Surprise and violence of action can overcome a lot. We'll be the only people leaving this house alive."

Ian swallowed. "For now. But the biggest risk isn't your enemy; it's the Handler."

Matz looked up from the floor plans, his eyes shifting first to me and then to Ian. The air conditioner kicked on with a rattle, and no one said anything until Ian spoke again.

"As soon as the war is won, you guys become a loose end—and he doesn't like loose ends."

Boss cleared his throat. "That's why the retirement plan is in place."

Ian nodded and stroked his chin thoughtfully. "I think you need to initiate that plan sooner than we thought. With all the work you guys have been doing, the opposition must be close to falling. It's only a matter of time before you kill a member of the senior leadership, and once the Five Heads start falling there's nothing standing in his way. How long before he's challenged again?"

"Ten years. Twenty."

"I'd say closer to twenty. Meanwhile, he's got an obligation to protect the legitimate part of the operation, and as soon as it's more profitable to do business without a paramilitary element, he will. I think he's going to offer you guys a bigger payday than usual upon completion of the last mission, whatever that may be. You need to take the deposit, deliver on the job, and leave without collecting the balance."

"Why are you so worried now?"

Ian hesitated. "Jimmy's team dropped off the map last week."

Ophie answered, "They made it to the Dominican."

"I heard that, too. But my guys didn't move them there. Who else would they trust?"

Matz shrugged. "Jimmy didn't trust anyone. I could see him setting up his own way out to be safe."

"And I hope they're all on the beach right now laughing at us. But all I know is they missed a meeting with their account manager from my side, and they haven't shown up since. Our recovery network is spun up because we can't rule out the possibility that they had a Midnight contingency."

"And that contingency means... what?" I asked.

Matz replied, "The word 'Midnight' over the radio means we've been set up. Everyone splits. No pickup, no Go To Hell points, just get as far as possible from whatever we planned. At that point, it's every man for himself."

"And then what?"

"There's a phone number for the recovery network. Back to the point—"

"Well, can I get the number?" I asked.

"Yeah, I'll hook you up. Don't be a pussy. Back to the point. Boss, this house is going to take some work. We're not going to be able to spare anyone."

Boss looked to Ian. "Can you get us a driver?"

"Our communications truck will be able to handle sniper placement and assault force drop-off. But after that, the truck will have to move to high ground for us to jam law enforcement frequencies and relay to you guys during the hit. Between that and me exploiting the van, I won't have anyone in the area available for pickup."

Ophie said, "That's a piece of cake—Special K is standing by. Waiting for our call in this very hotel, I believe."

"We need someone reliable," Matz said.

"You can say a lot of things about Special K, but unreliable isn't one of them."

"Fuck you."

Boss looked at Matz. "He's right. Make the call."

Ophie grinned.

14

The air was thick with the smell of pine needles and wet leaves as the house materialized in front of us. I waved away a cloud of insects from my face with a gloved hand and felt my breath quickening and my pulse racing as Boss's voice crackled through my ear.

"*Two minutes.*"

"Copy," Matz transmitted next to me, his voice echoing through my dual earpieces with a fraction of a second delay. Shifting his M4 assault rifle to the opposite hand, he leaned toward me and whispered, "There's a guy posted at the second floor window, left side. Hundred-meter shot. Take him on the two count and I'll get this other shithead standing by the back door."

"Got it." Feeling a slight tremor in my hands, I pretended to adjust the weight of my body armor, which, like Matz's, was neatly lined with ammunition and grenade pouches. I looked to see if he had noticed my hands shaking, but his eyes were studying the back of the house and flickering with excitement.

Ian trailed unseen behind us, his presence evidenced by an occasional branch snapping underfoot. Boss's figure moved through the brush to our left, his own M4 strapped to his back. He held the dual pistol grips of a semi-automatic grenade launcher with a stubby barrel that extended from a wide drum containing six 40mm high-explosive rounds.

Matz stalked forward in a low crouch before kneeling and transmitting, "Assault is at last cover and concealment. David's got a shot on the West A1 window and I've got one at West B3. No change to plan."

"*One minute,*" Boss replied. "*Ophie what do you got?*"

"*Front side of the house is quiet except for one guy posted at the East A3 window. I'll tag him on the two count. Sniper out.*"

Matz whispered to me, "How are you doing?"

I couldn't answer him honestly.

In truth, I was far more scared now than I had ever been in combat. After seeing the odds these guys would willingly take on, I felt little consolation that I wouldn't be alone this time as we assaulted a house containing six men. Once our meeting with Ian had adjourned, I returned to my hotel room and lay awake on the bed, my mind racing with likely outcomes of the upcoming mission and finding few positives.

I hadn't voiced my concerns to the others; instead, I took part in the preparations and rehearsals with a steadfast air of obedience to make up for ignoring Boss's order on the previous hit. To be sure, though, my act wasn't just about rebuilding their confidence in me. I had committed to their path no matter the cost. Weighed against the certainty of death by my own hand, the likelihood of death alongside the team was the lesser of two evils.

"I've never felt better," I said with indifference. "Let's kill these motherfuckers."

Matz slapped me on the shoulder so hard I had to steady myself against a tree. "That's what the fuck I'm talking about, Suicide. Between Boss's launcher and our hand grenades, the interior doors will be blown apart—or close to it. We should be able to kick down everything else, so leave that shotgun on your back unless I tell you to breach with it."

"*Thirty seconds.*"

"Stay behind me and hit your corners. Just like back at the house, only this time we get to shoot people. Don't worry about how many guys they have. What did I tell you before we left?"

"That we're only outgunned as long as we're missing."

"*Ten seconds.*"

Matz sighed wistfully. "God, I love my job. Now go."

Rising slowly above the brush, I wrapped my left hand around the tree trunk to my front, thumb pointed out, and rested the M4 handguard in the notch of my palm. Taking a breath, I rotated until I saw a figure in the second floor window—our first opponent. The hair on the back of my neck stood on end as I raised the reticle of my sight to his abdomen.

The figure darted out of view before I could fire.

"Compromised!" I said.

Matz's unsuppressed M4 split the quiet air like thunder.

I fired five shots through the now-empty window, hearing the dull *thump* of Boss's grenade launcher to my left as dogs began barking frantically throughout the subdivision. As I shifted aim and shot five more rounds, a back window of the house lit with a flash of orange. The sound of the explosion hit us a moment later.

Matz took off running through the underbrush. I fought through bushes and vines as I followed him, struggling to keep up while changing magazines.

We burst out of the woods and onto neatly trimmed grass as Boss fired a second grenade. The porch's sliding glass door vanished in a cloud of smoke and flame as we began our final sprint across the backyard.

I couldn't believe how fast Matz was running; he was almost twice my size, but I could barely keep up with him as he yelled with no shortness of breath, "Breach is clear!"

Two second floor windows flashed with fire, and fragments of glass rained onto the lawn. Matz withdrew a single hand grenade and hurled it through the remains of the elevated back door to our front, then cut right toward the porch steps.

I heard the detonation as we ran up the wooden stairs, and by the time I reached the porch Matz had already disappeared into the hollow doorway.

I launched myself into the house. The interior was a choking, swirling cloud of smoke, and Matz's figure was only dimly visible three long paces ahead of me. Swinging my barrel left, I fired into a charred body before looking right into an empty kitchen. I heard chaotic footsteps and men shouting on the second floor before Matz opened fire on the staircase.

"Take front!" he yelled to me, stepping to the side to reload as I passed him and posted myself at the base of the stairs. I fired at the shallow landing between the first and second floors until he squeezed my shoulder. He appeared beside me and climbed two steps to throw a grenade over the top of the staircase.

I changed magazines, glancing left to see Ian rushing through the back door, pistol in hand on his way to the garage. Then I flinched at the sudden explosion above us, its ear-splitting blast reverberating off the walls.

Matz followed the sound upward as it receded, then pivoted where the stairs turned and crouched down to fire toward the second floor landing in rapid succession. Bullets impacted the drywall several feet over his head, and the register of a distant rifle barked as he said, "Frag front."

I was vaguely aware of him changing magazines as I pulled a grenade from my vest. In the time it took me to yank the pin and throw it onto the second floor landing, Matz's voice came over the radio.

"*Support hit West A1, I say again hit—*"

An explosion from Boss's grenade launcher rocked the room at the top of the stairs, followed by my own grenade detonating on the landing a moment later.

Matz was managing the assault like an orchestra conductor.

He charged up the final few stairs, shooting to his front before breaking right. I followed a step behind him, firing at muzzle flashes from the corner of an open doorway before the enemy shooter rolled behind cover. Cutting right to back up Matz, I flowed into the master bedroom to find him turning left and shooting into a shattered closet doorway.

An otherworldly two-second burping noise rang out from within the closet, and Matz dropped like a stone, puffs of crimson suspended in his wake. I didn't make it a step toward the closet before a monster of a man strode out of it, his eyes ablaze within a wide, bearded face.

His meat hook of a hand released a now-empty machine pistol. It fell to the floor as he charged me.

I wildly raised my M4, shooting as fast as I could pull the trigger and walking four rounds up his chest. The last impacted just below his collarbone before he tackled me to the ground.

My rifle was pinned flat against my chest as wide, sweaty palms encircled my throat and squeezed with unbelievable strength. His eyes were wild with rage and small rivers of blood streamed from both ears.

I reached for my pistol and found it wedged beneath my hip, so I drew the knife from my vest instead. He grabbed my wrist with one hand and slammed it to the ground, continuing to choke me as the other maintained his weight on my throat.

I panicked, desperately trying to shove my free thumb into his eye as he pulled back his head. Then I punched weakly at his throat as my brain screamed for air. Blood slammed against the inside of my skull and my vision narrowed into an ever-tightening circle; at the periphery, I saw another bodyguard approaching from outside the bedroom and holding a raised submachine gun. He saw his comrade on top of me and angled his barrel into the doorway, stepping sideways to clear the room.

His head vanished under a geyser of smoke and he fell out of sight.

Matz appeared over me, his M4 hanging on the sling as he clutched a knife in an icepick grip. Leaning over my attacker, he slid the blade into the base of the giant's skull. The last thing I saw was the man's face frozen in death, but his hands remained fixed on my throat and wrist. All at once, the pressure in my head seemed to evaporate and I passed out.

I awoke suddenly, instinctively taking flustered, seizing gasps of air. For seconds, I had no idea where I was or how I got there. The massive man's corpse lay stiffly on the ground beside me.

Matz said, "Suicide, get up and quit fucking around."

Through fluttering eyelids, I saw him standing in the doorway with his M4 at the ready. My earpieces filled with his voice transmitting, "*Boss, I need you on the second floor. Link up at the top of the stairs.*"

"*Moving.*"

I coughed my way back to life, rolling over on all fours and struggling to rise.

Matz continued, "*Sniper, what's your body count?*"

Ophie answered, "*I tagged one guard in the garage, but the guy in East A3 squirted before the two count. No Joy.*"

I shakily rose to my feet, falling onto the bed and stabbing the mattress with the knife I'd forgotten was clutched in my hand. Inserting it into its sheath, I struggled upright and regained my equilibrium. I stumbled to Matz's backside, then squeezed his shoulder and gasped, "I'm up."

"Good for you. Reload your fucking weapon." I changed magazines as he continued, "There's one PA and the fat-ass primary left, so if you die after this, it's your fault."

"Okay," I wheezed.

From the stairway to our left, Boss called, "EAGLE EAGLE EAGLE."

With that, Matz moved out of the doorway and swung right, with me trailing behind him. We crossed the open landing as I heard Boss vault a final step and follow us. I sped up and pivoted right at the corner to cover a closed doorway. Matz and Boss flowed past me to enter the room to my left.

I turned and followed them inside the empty room, stopping behind Boss as he posted beside the open doorway on the right. Beyond it, a shared bathroom adjoined the last remaining bedroom; Matz delivered a grenade into it with a light underhand toss.

We ducked against the wall as the explosive detonated, the concussion close enough to momentarily suck the air from our lungs. Boss moved forward, hooking right as I swung left and almost ran into a destroyed desk. What used to be a large window was now lined only with a few shards of remaining glass, and through it I caught a glimpse of the wooded hill from which we had approached minutes earlier.

Before I could collapse my sector toward Boss, Matz was already at his side firing rounds into the base of a closet door.

I saw a bloody smear at my feet that extended into the closet.

"DON'T SHOOT, DON'T SHOOT!" came a frantic cry from within.

I knelt and fired six rounds, stitching them back and forth across the closet door. Then I nodded to Matz, who approached the door from the side and opened it.

The personal assistant was curled on the floor.

He made frightened breathing sounds, holding both of his hands open in front of his face, his right shoulder and leg torn open and bleeding profusely. Shrapnel and bullet wounds covered his body as he squinted up at us.

Matz yelled, "Where is he?"

"I—I don't—"

"Wrong answer," Matz said, shooting twice into the dying man's knees.

He screamed, "ATTIC!"

Matz shot him in the bridge of his nose and his head flung back. Then

Matz led the way back to the master bedroom. We crossed the landing as dust-clouded sunlight streamed through broken blinds and glass, neatly outlining a body with a clean headshot that splayed his brain across the carpet.

Matz stepped over the body of the dead giant— the knife handle still protruded from his skull—and faced the open closet door on the left. He fired around a square hatch in the ceiling, emptying his magazine, then called, "Switch."

I picked up where he had left off, peppering the untouched sections of the bedroom ceiling. We heard a sudden cry of pain from a far corner, and Matz fired a second full magazine toward the noise as I reloaded, squatted down, and braced my back against the closet wall under the attic hatch.

He finished his reload and approached me with his barrel pointed upward, holding it with one hand as he placed a boot on my knee. He stepped up, his immense weight applied momentarily to my knee, then took another step onto my shoulder as he opened the hatch above him and hoisted himself up with a grace I hadn't believed possible.

He vanished into the black space above me.

Boss and I heard thumping in the attic, followed by Matz muttering, "Let's go, shithead."

The primary target's round, sweating face appeared in the open hatch, his eyes wild with fear. Matz maneuvered him until his body came crashing to the closet floor.

Sliding my M4 to my back, I grabbed him under the arms and dragged him into the bedroom as he screamed, "GET OFF OF ME! DON'T FUCKING TOUCH ME!"

I released him on the floor, my gloves coming away bloody from his bullet wounds. Matz jumped down as Boss took a picture of the man's face.

"That's payday," he said.

Matz fired his M4 three times into the man's head, stepping back for Boss to take another picture before patting down the body. He withdrew a cell phone from the target's pocket and deposited it into a dump pouch on his hip, then grabbed the giant's empty machine pistol from the ground and did the same.

Boss transmitted, "Net call, JACKPOT JACKPOT JACKPOT. Assault and Support moving to pickup."

"*Sniper copies*," Ophie replied.

I turned to the massive body of the man who had choked me and pulled the knife out of his neck, then handed it to Matz. He reinserted it into his vest and led the way out of the house, limping down the stairs.

As we set foot on the ground floor, the door to the garage swung open and Ian staggered forward, his pistol in his hand and a duffel bag on his back, looking as excited as a child on Christmas morning.

"They had so much shit in that van and I got it all. You have no idea. Also, the cops will be here any second—no rush."

We trotted into the bright sunshine of the back porch as the wail of police sirens approached, and Boss snatched his grenade launcher from the wall at the breach point. Neighborhood dogs were still barking from all directions as we crossed to the edge of the yard, fighting our way into the underbrush to disappear into the woods. Running through thick foliage as the ground softened underfoot, we splashed through a narrow creek and ascended up a wooded hill as the police sirens grew fainter.

We ran on a due west course toward our pickup site, covering ground as quickly as the vegetation and Matz's limp would allow. Once we crested the hill and moved down the opposite side, Boss stopped us. He put pressure dressings on Matz's arms as Matz slid a tourniquet into place high on his right thigh.

The entire process was over within a minute.

"David, take point," Boss said. "Ian, you cover the back. Let's move."

He helped Matz to his feet, supporting his weight as he limped forward.

I led the way through the woods as the others trailed behind. After walking several hundred meters, I glimpsed the dirt construction road through the trees.

I transmitted, "Stop movement, I have eyes on the road."

"*Copy*."

I crouched lower and crept forward as I identified the silver SUV. The driver was leaning against the front quarter panel, looking bored and smoking a cigarette. I watched for a few seconds, then took a breath and transmitted over the radio.

"Boss, our driver must have been killed by some kind of stunning ethereal goddess. I'm getting in the car anyway."

Matz immediately replied, *"FUCK you, Suicide. I'll stab you in the head just like that fucking guard—"*

I pulled out my earpieces and strode into the open.

She had the frame of a gymnast, petite and slender and carried with an effortless grace. Shoulder-length blonde hair fell sharply around her face and was jetted with streaks of dark pink. As the long cloud of cigarette smoke began to dissipate, I saw her clear blue eyes and pale pink lipstick.

I extended my hand and smiled. "Hi, I'm David Rivers."

She casually transferred her cigarette to her left hand and shook mine. Her slim arm was tattooed from the wrist up with cherry blossoms and colorful Koi fish.

"Where's Matz?" she asked.

"Taking his time. Seems he got himself shot."

"Is he all right?"

"He'll be fine."

"Too bad. Cigarette?"

"Those things will kill you."

She examined my eyes humorlessly. "Your face is covered in blood."

"On second thought, I'd love one... Special K?"

"Karma."

"Of course."

The others emerged from the woods. Matz hissed, "Get in the fucking car," as Boss assisted him into the vehicle. Ian unslung his bag and got in behind them. Karma watched them with a neutral expression, then rotated the cigarette in her hand and, holding it backwards between her thumb and forefinger, raised it to my lips.

I leaned forward and took a single draw, tasting her lipstick on the filter and pulling smoke into lungs that only minutes ago were deprived of oxygen. Suppressing the urge to cough, I exhaled coolly. "Until next time, Karma."

I got into the back, and Karma slid herself into the driver's seat. Closing the door behind her, she started the car and pulled forward.

Matz ordered, "Pick up Ophie and then detour to the medical point."

Karma slammed on the brakes, jolting everyone forward in their seats.

She glared at him in the rearview mirror. "Oh, is that what we're doing? I thought you wanted to bleed out on the way to the airport after leaving Ophie behind."

"Nice to see you, Karma!" Ian said with a grin.

I added, "You're beautiful, Karma."

"Stop talking right now," Matz said. "Both of you."

The truck lurched forward once again. Boss said nothing, but I could see a rare smile of amusement on his face. We rolled down the bumpy dirt path until the construction trail met the paved street of a neighborhood, and then took a right turn toward the main road.

* * *

The roll-up door to the storage unit slid open as we approached, and Karma navigated into it. A severe-looking elderly man waved us forward, crossing his arms to stop us once the SUV was fully inside. Karma killed the engine and we exited into a narrow space. The unit was deep enough to fit a second truck, but the remaining area was packed with two folding tables and metal shelves lined with medical supplies. Yellow work lights mounted atop tripod stands lit the interior, and lengths of extension cords ran along the floor.

"Casualty to me," the old man directed. "Close that door, and our man will lock it from the outside. Don't step outside the unit or you'll be on camera." Ian pulled down the door, the shrill scraping sound echoing inside the concrete space.

Ophie and I helped Matz out of the truck and led him toward the tables.

The man asked, "Any symptoms or treatments since you called?"

"No," Matz said.

"Get his equipment off and set him on the table."

Ophie unclipped Matz's armored vest and carefully lifted it from his shoulders. The front was peppered with bullets, their round holes neatly bored into his spare magazines and armored plate.

Ophie gave a low whistle. "Looks like you spit in God's face again."

I helped Matz onto the table and stepped back as the man approached him with a stethoscope.

"Czechoslovakia's finest," Ophie said admiringly. I turned to see him holding the machine pistol he had pulled from Matz's dump pouch. "This is the new one?"

Matz replied, "Yeah. The charging handle on the old one was—"

"Gentlemen," the old man barked in a hoarse tone. "I need to get a set of vitals. No talking from the casualty, and the rest of you please keep it down. This is a commercial facility."

"This is a family restaurant," Karma said in a husky imitation of the man's tone. "No talking from the bullet magnet."

Ophie set down the machine pistol and turned to her. "You are such a bitch."

"Just trying to blend in with the present company."

"How did the art show go?"

"Unfortunately, not well enough to turn down this stellar use of my time. Trust me, Ophie, the day I've got enough to retire is the day I stop answering your calls whenever you guys need a winsome driver to cart you around."

The doctor murmured to himself as he treated Matz. Blood poured from the wounds as he removed the pressure dressings Boss had applied.

"When we get married," Ophie told her, "I'll buy everything you ever paint."

"You've never seen my work."

"Semantics. Boss tells me you're coming back to the house."

"Imagine my enthusiasm."

I turned to see Ian laying his duffel bag on the ground in front of the SUV. He crouched over it, powered on a laptop with decryption software, and began going through the bag. He plugged in a portable hard drive as Boss joined him, taking a knee and whispering to him.

Ophie continued, "Well, look on the bright side: you're moonlighting as the highest paid taxi driver in the world."

"Just what every girl dreams of."

"There can only be so many jobs left before we're done."

"You guys said that a year ago."

"Now we mean it." He looked over at me. "David, have you and Karma been formally introduced?"

I answered, "We had a very deep and meaningful human connection at the pickup site."

"You just stay away from her, if you know what's good for you," Ophie said. "She's already promised herself to me if she ever returns to men."

She shook her head. "How many times do I have to explain I'm not a lesbian? You know what? Let's keep pretending I am; it would give me some peace and quiet during these little excursions."

I heard Ian whisper a sharp, "Holy FUCK," and turned to see him staring into the laptop's glowing screen. Then, he said to Boss, "You need to get this hard drive to him."

"To who?" Boss said.

"Him. You need to send it to him because I'm sure as shit not going to."

Boss squinted at the screen. "What is it?"

"Retirement. These are the account numbers the Five Heads are using to launder money for their organization."

"So what?"

"So these accounts are the only thing isolating their legitimate financiers from the illegal part of the operation. If they're exposed, a lot of people very high up on the food chain will be caught benefiting from the outlaws."

"You think the Handler can use this to force the Five Heads into negotiations?"

"I know he can. This is the key to destroying the entire organization without firing a single shot."

Boss gazed hollowly at the screen, but his expression remained placid. "All right. Let me know what else you find."

Ian unplugged the hard drive and set it to the side, then withdrew another one from his bag and plugged it in.

Boss rose and walked to the doctor. I waited until he passed before approaching Ian and kneeling beside him.

"Why are you so worried about the Handler?"

Ian performed a flurry of keystrokes on the computer, but didn't slow as he answered, "They don't believe me, do they?"

"I'm not going to lie to you, Ian. They make fun of you a little bit."

"I just don't want to see us destroyed by our own creator."

"How do you mean?"

Ian stopped typing and looked at me, as if gauging whether I was serious. "He invented us, David. No one hired special operations folks to kill the competition until he did, and then it became an arms race between organizations. And those only end one way."

"What kind of organizations?"

Boss snapped his fingers. "Ian. That's enough."

We looked up to see him standing over us. Behind him, Karma, who had been watching me closely, turned away. I rose, both knees popping.

"That's the third and final bullet," the doctor announced, holding a bloody piece of metal between the tined ends of his forceps.

As he began dressing the entry wound, Boss asked, "How's he doing, Doc?"

"He was hit in both arms and the right leg, all three only resulting in muscular damage. You can do the math on how many rounds his front plate and soft armor took without failing. He should buy a lottery ticket."

Ophie responded, "We've tried the lottery tickets before—turns out his luck is dog shit unless he's getting shot at."

"What's his recovery looking like?" Boss asked.

"He needs three weeks of bed rest to let his leg heal."

Matz snorted. "Well, I've heard that before."

The elderly doctor looked at him. "After that, limited activity for another few months. You're looking at four months, maybe five, until he fully recovers. That's if you take recuperation seriously. If not, it could be much longer."

"Thanks, Doc," Boss said. "You have a pack for him?"

The doctor grabbed a paper bag from the shelf and handed it to Boss.

"Antibiotics, disinfectant, and additional dressings. The wounds will need to be cleaned and evaluated daily—you guys know the drill. At a minimum, get him reevaluated weekly by a doctor until the wounds start healing over."

"We'll see to it, Doc."

We changed into clean civilian clothes and packed our weapons and equipment into the back of the truck. After Ian's men screened the route to the airport for police checkpoints, we loaded up and left the storage unit.

Once we got to the airport, Joe's plane was waiting.

* * *

I sat in my room with the lights out, hearing a toilet flush before the final door closed. We had arrived well after dark, and went to bed minutes after shuttling the boxes of equipment to the basement.

Once the house fell silent, I went to the kitchen.

Retrieving the bottle of Woodford and a short glass, I filled the latter a third of the way with ice. I poured bourbon to the very top and polished it off within a minute. Two more followed in short succession before I reached the trance-like state I would sustain like a Buddhist monk for the next three to four hours.

Pouring a fourth drink, I considered sitting at the oak table where the team had decided my fate after I killed Saamir. Then, thinking better of it, I turned off the light and went onto the back porch to watch the wide expanse of stars glow across a cloudless sky. The air was thick and heavy, and I settled into an old wooden chair with my glass, undeterred by the mosquitos flittering around my head.

I slowly sipped my bourbon, my mind restoring itself to a state of beautiful harmony amid the lucid, alcohol-laced memories of our firefight. My thoughts drifted from room to room in the house, from being crushed by the giant to emerging with our lives, marred by the blood of our enemies but ultimately victorious against forces of fate that seemed greater than we were.

The back door opened, and Karma stepped out onto the porch.

Nearby crickets fell silent as the door closed behind her, leaving only a distant chorus from the woods. She took a few steps and set a wine glass on the rail, then withdrew a cigarette from a shiny blue pack and slid it between her lips. I watched her raise the lighter to her mouth, the soft profile of her face lit in the flickering glow for just a moment, until all that remained in the blackness was the ember of her cigarette. She turned toward me and jumped.

"Hi, David. I didn't see you there."

"Hi, Karma."

She took a drag and blew the smoke sideways over the rail. "So how'd you get mixed up with the wayward boys here at the shittiest summer camp on the planet?"

"Mutual acquaintance." My mind drifted back to the image of Peter collapsed on the floor and begging for his life. "I could ask you the same thing. When they said Special K was coming, I wasn't sure what to expect."

"Well, when they said there was a new guy named Suicide, I anticipated someone over the age of eighteen."

"Twenty-five."

"Jesus. You're the youngest guy here by almost ten years. Here, I still owe you one of these." She produced another cigarette, lit it with her own, and handed it to me. I accepted it as she continued, "Matz tells me they pulled some kind of a bear gun off you because you were going to blow off your own head."

"Matz has a flair for the dramatic."

"He's not known for an overactive imagination. And he said you still might."

I took a drag, the smoke dancing in my lungs before I blew a cloud toward the dark forest. "Who knows?"

"You're still a kid, David. And you're not one of these guys yet, thank God. It's not too late for you to have a life outside of here." There was something infinitely sexy about her voice, a scratchiness that hummed along with her every thought, melodious.

"I might point out that you're standing here beside me."

"That's fair. God knows I've got my own circumstances, and I'm not trying to judge you. But you know the only thing that's the end of the world, David? The end of the world. You can recover from everything else, and you can't be putting a gun to your head every time something goes wrong in your life. Boss told me a little about your past. I know you don't have any family, but there's got to be something you can go back to."

"I'm not asking for your sympathy, Karma. Things turned out how they turned out, and I have no cause for complaint."

I took a drink while she watched me, smoke drifting through her parted lips. The nearby crickets resumed their chorus, but now pulsated out of rhythm with the song from the woods.

"I hope you find what you're looking for, David. I really do. But if you're like this now, I'm scared to think of how you'll be when you're as old as these guys. I see the way you look at them. You probably listen to them talk about how close they are to the end and how great everything will be in retirement, and you're buying it hook, line, and sinker."

"So what? They've earned it."

"Except they're going to be as unhappy down south as they are here. Maybe more. A mansion on the beach isn't going to change anything, if they make it that far. Once there are no more jobs and no one else to kill, they're going to see how empty they are inside. All that inner hatred won't suddenly go away because there are palm trees around."

"Then why did you tell Ophie you will be coming with them?"

Lowering the glass to her waist, the liquid swishing inside, her unblinking eyes watched me for several long seconds.

"You really don't get it. I'll be able to come back to America, David. No one knows who I am. And unless the cops pin the Saamir job on you, they probably won't know you, either. But Matz and Ophie and Boss are in too deep, and people would be trying to kill them their entire lives if they stayed here. You think they're living in this house in the middle of nowhere because they can plug back into society whenever they want? Caspian went home to see his mom when she got her diagnosis and he disappeared within a week. There's no going back for them. Retiring down south is their only solution to the one problem they can't kill. So, yes, I'm going to help you guys move. And after that, I'll keep visiting to make sure that all of you are okay, because I'm terrified that you won't be."

Her eyes turned toward the sky for a moment, and then she flung the remaining few sips of wine off the porch. She took a final drag from her cigarette and threw that off, too.

Without looking back, she said, "Goodnight, David."

"Goodnight, Karma."

She vanished, leaving me as she found me.

CONDEMNED

A fronte praecipitium a tergo lupi

-A precipice in front, wolves behind

15

Boss's phone rang at lunch the next day. He always carried two, though I had never seen him receive a call on the second one.

"Send it," he said, followed by a long pause. "Good afternoon, sir." He snapped his fingers and pointed toward a pen and paper. I set them in front of him.

"Yes, sir, go ahead." He began scrawling, and I struggled to follow his cryptic shorthand. Above a single line of text, he wrote *FIVE*. "Understood. That won't be a problem, sir. We're on it." After another long pause, Boss smiled. "Sir, if this call could be traced, we wouldn't be the team you wanted... Yes, sir."

He hung up and looked at us.

Ophie said, "Sounded like that went well."

"Looks like the information Ian pulled out of that van paid off, after all. The Five Heads have a meeting in two weeks to figure out how to prevent exposure. We've got a date and a time, but no location other than somewhere in Colorado. And that was the Handler himself, not his assistant."

Matz asked, "All of them will be there at the same time? That doesn't make sense."

"They must be getting desperate. Ophie, spin up Joe for an out-of-state flight; total weight will be double the last job, if not more, and we'll get him the details as soon as we have them. Matz, take David and start getting all the team gear loaded and ready for transport. I'm bringing in Ian."

"What's the mission?" I asked.

Boss looked at me with a vacant stare. "To kill them all."

* * *

The next day, a single car drove slowly up the long dirt driveway. Its lone occupant parked in front of the house and stumbled out of the vehicle before grabbing a carry-on bag from the trunk.

Ophie, watching from the front door, yelled, "Coffee! Get this man coffee!"

I poured a cup and returned to see Ian staggering inside with his satchel slung over one shoulder. His eyes were bloodshot, set over black rings.

Matz said, "What the fuck happened to you?"

"I haven't slept since I got the call. We found the site. Let me brief you guys, and then I'm going to pass out for a few hours while you start planning."

Boss asked, "Do you want to lie down first? You look like shit."

"It's big. You guys need to get started now."

Ian arranged maps and photographs on the kitchen table, and we crowded around him. He drank half the cup of steaming coffee in a series of long sips before setting down the mug. Then, he removed a round tin from his pocket, pinched out a small amount of brown powder, and snorted it. After repeating the process with the opposite nostril, he closed the tin and put it in his pocket.

"Okay, let's get started," he said. "The meeting will take place within this walled compound." He pointed to a photograph of an overhead view. "Pretty remote—used to be a private estate, and now it's rented out for private events and rich businessmen to fuck their mistresses. As you can see, we've got a main building, guesthouse, and pool house next to—"

"Was that cocaine?" I asked.

"What? No, just nasal snuff."

"David," Boss said, "shut up. Ian, go ahead."

"So this compound is something of a retreat, set out in rolling hills with a scenic view. The main drive runs out to a two-lane hardball, and most of the surrounding area is crisscrossed with dirt roads. The Handler was right: each of the Five Heads will be there on the date he specified. Since they all operate independently, their personal security details will escort them to and from the site once the inner and outer security rings are set.

"The inner security ring will start with a full sweep of the site, which means counter surveillance for listening devices and bomb dogs sniffing for explosives. Once it's clean, they'll be strong-pointing the compound and controlling access in and out. We can safely assume they'll conduct roving patrols into the dead space within five hundred meters or so of the compound.

"A third-party company will set up the outer security ring. That will include blocking access routes while the meeting is underway and conducting vehicle patrols along the surrounding roads. I'd also bank on them having observation posts for every major intersection within two kilometers. Anything suspicious will result in a call for one of their vehicles to check it out."

Boss asked, "How many security guys in each of the rings?"

"Too many. We don't have a number yet, but it's going to be a lot. More than you can take on directly."

Ophie said, "I believe the doctrinal term is a 'metric fuck-ton.'"

Matz looked at Ian. "Can we hit the principal vehicles on the way in or out?"

"You could cherry-pick one or two, but you won't get them all. Their arrival and departure will be staggered."

Boss said, "Their departure won't be staggered if a ground assault initiates an evacuation. They'll be fighting each other to be first out the gate, and if their drivers are worth a shit—which they are—they'll be bumper-to-bumper on the way out with the lead vehicle setting the speed. That puts them in a single convoy, ripe for the picking. Is the third-party security responsible for evacuation?"

"No, that'll fall on their personal security details. The auxiliary security would cover the area while the principals are loaded and shipped out."

"So it'll have the added benefit of leaving most of the guards at the compound. And the convoy"—he pointed at the map—"will have to traverse this stretch of road to the next major intersection before they can split up. What if we set an ambush along that, maybe at a turn where they naturally slow down? Explosives alone could do the trick if we're lucky. Throw in a few guys with rocket launchers and a medium machine gun, and it'd be a sure thing."

"That's a hardball road," Ian pointed out. "You're not going to be able to dig in and place an IED."

Matz leaned forward, setting his fists on the table. "We could still dig under it, and if we use enough explosives along the side of the road it won't even matter. I'm talking P is for plenty, Fourth of July, total destruction, overkill to the highest degree. The last thing we need is for some security vehicles interspersed in the convoy to eat the blast and let a principal escape."

"Even so, when would you dig it in? The outer security ring will be patrolling that area."

Boss replied, "Not a week before the meeting, they won't. We could go in early, identify the best kill zone, and bury our explosives during a period of darkness. Hell, we could bury the rockets and machine gun, too, and then camouflage everything and leave. Before the meeting takes place, we do a vehicle drop-off outside their security perimeter and move quietly through the woods to the ambush site."

Matz asked, "But how do we get them to evacuate in the first place?"

"Mortars should do the trick."

"What are mortars?" Karma chimed in.

Ophie cut his eyes toward her. "That's what you get for bringing a woman into a man's work, boys. Karma, mortars are those big tubes on a bipod you might remember from every war movie you've ever seen in your goddamn life. One guy adjusts the angle and another drops in a round, the tube goes boom, and something far away gets blown up."

"Got it." Karma nodded.

Ian shook his head. "Boss, if they receive indirect fire they're more likely to hunker down and wait it out. They'll know you don't have unlimited rounds."

Boss closed his eyes and inhaled. "Not if we convince them they're going to be overrun."

Matz replied, "We don't have enough guys to do a ground assault. Not by a long shot."

"They don't know that, and these guys are even more terrified of the Handler than Ian is. If we start dropping 120mm mortar rounds, then switch to 81mm and then 60mm, shifting fire as we go, that'll be pretty fucking convincing that a ground force is moving in from the opposite direction. They'll evacuate any principals left alive, right toward our ambush. And if they don't evacuate at all, then they're stationary, and we'll put every mortar round we can into their position and leave as planned. If anyone survives, we police them up in secondary hits once Ian can pinpoint their locations."

Ian leaned forward, resting his elbows on the table. "Tactical plan sounds feasible, if you can man it. The secondary hits are where I disagree. My strongest recommendation is that you retire after this mission, no matter the outcome. Leave the final payment and make this the last job you do. Boss, did the Handler tell you how he knew the date and time of the meeting?"

Karma stood, holding a fist pensively under her chin. Her eyes met mine, and I looked to Boss.

"No," Boss said. "He didn't."

"He's been in talks with the Five Heads. The account information from that Sprinter van on the last target drove them to negotiations, just like I told you it would. Now, the Five Heads and their organization are considering peace terms ranging from a friendly merger all the way to just buying their way out of being hunted. The details are being finalized that day. Did he tell you any of that, Boss?"

"No."

"Then he also didn't mention that he's going to be on a conference call with the Five Heads at that meeting."

"No."

"Exactly. He's playing along with the negotiations just to get them consolidated so he can send you guys in for a decapitation strike. He doesn't care about the potential for financial gain or expansion, no matter how many tens or hundreds of millions in profit that may earn over the long term. And we know by now that he is a very long-term planner. What does that tell you?"

Boss replied, "He's setting a precedent."

Ian nodded slowly. "The world isn't big enough to hide his enemies. A challenge to his organization is an open-ended death contract that can't be bought or backed out of. If the other side had been successful, I have no doubt that he would have taken it to the point of mutually assured destruction, and that's not because he isn't calculated."

"Then why is it?" Matz asked.

"I think he's like you guys, in a way. He's chosen his path, and he's committed himself to it at the exclusion of all else. He's done his time in the trenches, and now he's the one moving the chess pieces. And I think he enjoys it. If I were trying to recruit him as a source, I would offer him more of what he's doing. Not money, not women. I don't believe in evil, but I think this man is as close to that force as you're going to encounter in this lifetime."

Ophie straightened his arms up and outward in a long stretch. "Hopefully evil pays, because I'm ready to start working on my tan. And stop with all the melodrama, Ian. You're scaring Karma."

Ian frowned. "Finish this target and leave upon completion. Skip the final payment and call it a day. He's going to have a list of secondary targets to clean up, no matter how many you kill at the meeting, but you'll never get to the end of that list."

I asked, "Then why not bail now?"

Matz answered, "If we don't complete this job, we're as good as dead. Once we finish the work, he won't pursue us. Taking the deposit and leaving the remainder of our final payment is a standard assurance that we're gone for good, and that's the only way you get out of this game without dying. Ophie, where would you set up a mortar point?"

Ian leaned back and folded his arms, looking first to Karma and then to me, but remained silent.

Ophie studied the map and pointed to a spot. "I'd say somewhere on this hill. That's about three kilometers from the target, so it's pushing it for the 60mm range, but easy money for the 81 and 120. Any farther and you're losing the 60; any closer and you're within the outer security ring."

Matz said, "We'll have to do the same thing we have planned for the ambush site. Dial in the mortars to the target, waterproof the cannons and the rounds, camouflage everything, and then come back to it right before the hit."

"What about our getaway?" Ophie asked. "Based on the location of the mortar firing point and the ambush position, we'll need a separate driver for each element."

Boss said, "I'd add a third, driving a vehicle big enough to fit the entire team. We could stage it at a three-way intersection of these narrow dirt roads and have everyone move to that point. The other two cars can park sideways on the roads they came in on, blocking them to vehicle traffic to slow down any pursuers. That has the added benefit of providing some flexibility when we leave: if one element can't make the link-up on time, then we've still blocked the opposite road access without slowing their movement along the main escape route."

Ian said, "I can provide two drivers, including myself."

"Special K will be the third. That leaves the four of us, and since we'll need at least three at the ambush site, I'd say David's on mortars by himself."

"Why not Matz?" I asked. "His leg is still healing."

Ophie replied, "All the more reason he needs to be with Boss and me. If anything falls through on our end, there are three of us all jacked on adrenaline. Matz isn't going to be left behind; we'll make it happen one way or the other. I can get the mortars dialed in when we move the equipment, so long as David can hang the rounds."

Ian said, "You need more people. Sending in David alone is crazy, and three guys against five cars is fucking ludicrous. You almost lost David and Matz on that last hit, and that was only against four guards. Bring in some hired guns on this one."

The table fell silent. Boss picked up the compound imagery in one hand and the map in the other, his eyes moving between them. He set them back down, then looked at the faces across from him. Matz gave a slight nod. Ophie remained expressionless.

Boss said, "We can handle it."

"How?" Ian asked. "Just hire more guys to mitigate your risk to force."

Matz answered, "A few more guys is a few more pay cuts. We've got enough shares as it is, especially since David has failed to die."

Boss said, "Bringing in outside guys is risky, especially if we're approaching the end of our useful life with the Handler. It'd be tough to vet anyone in this time frame."

Karma's eyes were lively with disbelief. "So you're risking total annihilation to stack money higher than you already have? Brilliant."

"No one's forcing you to be here," Matz said in a flat voice. "You know the terms."

"Yeah, and I keep coming back to watch you push it just a little further. But one of these times, it's going to be too far."

Ian said, "Boss, your getaway on this should take you straight to retirement. I'm serious. Pack up the house beforehand, and we'll ship whatever you want. Don't come back after the hit. I'll drive the main getaway vehicle myself, and we'll pull into the back of an eighteen-wheeler once we get away and put you in the pipeline south."

"I'm okay with that," Matz said.

Ophie shrugged. "Me too."

Boss asked, "Is anyone outside this room tracking David's involvement yet?"

Ian shook his head. "No. They haven't been able to piece him together with Saamir's death. And they've pretty much given up on Peter's murder, which is all the more reason David should go with you: as long as he doesn't get burned before retirement, he can liaise back to the States for anything you guys need."

I nodded. "I'll rack up frequent flyer miles for you guys."

Boss steepled his fingers, his tired eyes settling individually on every person in the room. They lingered on me the longest as he considered Ian's words. Drawing a deep breath while the rest of us held ours, he finally said, "Let's set it up."

Ian replied, "Got it. Are you guys good with this information for now? I'd like to go to the spirit world for a while."

"We're good," Boss said. "Crash in my room for as long as you like. We'll be here for a while."

Ian took his satchel and left the kitchen.

Boss announced, "Okay, let's red cell this so far. What issues do we have?"

Ophie grunted. "Well, here's a big one that Ian's missing: setting the explosives will require us to park on a hardball road, so there won't be any tracks on the ground besides what we can cover up in the woods. Likewise, before the hit, the three of us can drop off on a hardball and walk in without crossing any dirt roads."

"Agreed. So?"

"Well, take a look at the mortar point. Closest drop-off is a dirt road, so between the vehicle tracks and the equipment offload into the woods, we're going to leave plenty of ground disturbance for a security team to find."

"Mitigated by setting up early and bypassing all dirt roads afterwards."

"We're going to have to drop off David somewhere, and this spider web of dirt roads all around the hill can't be avoided. The farther he moves on foot, the more danger he's in. We're pushing the known limits of the outer security ring as it is, and David would be in danger of being spotted by an observation post every time he crossed a road, or by someone finding his tracks. Either scenario would point them straight to the mortar site."

Boss studied the map while massaging his temple.

I asked, "Boss, can I see that?"

He handed it to me.

Matz said, "Here we go. Let's see what you come up with, Suicide. What did you learn in college that's going to help us out here?"

"Not a goddamn thing. But I know what I can do with a parachute. You've got a small clearing on this ridge about a kilometer from the mortar point, and it's inside all the dirt road boundaries. Even with scattered trees, that's ample space for me to land."

"Maybe if you're jumping from a few hundred feet, but not out of a plane."

"I'd be opening at a few hundred feet. This would be with BASE gear, not a skydiving rig. Unless you want them to see a parachute at three thousand feet that circles for a few minutes before landing."

Boss said, "I'm more concerned with a plane flying overhead and a guy falling out of it right next to our mortar point."

"Have Joe offset by three kilometers. Let me jump from fourteen thousand feet with a wingsuit, and I'll fly right to it."

Karma said, "Well, this is no more ridiculous than any of the other great ideas we've discussed so far."

"What if you bounce?" Ophie asked.

I leaned back in my seat. "Let me jump the day before the hit. If I don't check in, you could bump Ophie from the ambush to risk walking to the mortars as a contingency. If I miss a subsequent check-in because security rolled me up, you could abort altogether. Either way, you've got one guy assuming the risk before you commit your entire ambush team and drivers."

Boss held out his open hand to me, and I gave him back the map.

Ophie asked, "You could fly that far with your squirrel suit?"

"Wingsuit. And yes."

Matz said, "I think you've seen too many James Bond movies."

I looked up at him. "If you have a better idea, Matz, let's hear it."

Boss stared at the map, saying nothing.

16

We touched down just before sunrise, the screech of our wheels as they hit the runway jarring me awake. I looked out the window at the mountains ringed by shimmering golden hues across the sky. Turning my head, I saw Karma watching me. She looked away. Ophie and Matz were still asleep, oblivious to our arrival. Boss hadn't slept at all.

Joe taxied the Caravan off the runway and into a private hangar. Two quad-cab pickups were parked in the corner of the open clamshell structure. The plane came to a halt, and Joe powered down the engine as we descended onto a concrete floor and prepared to unload our equipment.

The flight had been considerably dangerous, and the day ahead would be even more so. We had packed thousands of pounds of military grade hardware and explosives into a single vessel and flown it across state lines. Almost any item chosen at random from our cargo represented a life sentence in prison for possession alone, not including domestic terrorism charges.

Having only a single week to acquire and train on the necessary equipment stretched our time and resources. Not to mention the process of packing all of our worldly possessions, which added strain to our already packed schedule. Matz had managed our timeline down to the hour, and we were exhausted by the time we had finally finished loading the aircraft. Everyone besides Boss and Joe were asleep before takeoff.

The push wasn't over. The equipment that was risky for us to transport to a commercial airport was far riskier to move in pickup trucks for two and a half hours toward the remote target area, which necessitated daylight, and lots of it. We couldn't risk exposure at the ambush site, where the very act of burying and camouflaging the explosives alongside the road would likely be an all-night process. We would spend any remaining darkness hiding a cache of rocket launchers and the machine gun. After that, we wouldn't be able to return until the day of the meeting, by which time security would have been patrolling the area we'd already infiltrated.

It was a massive effort for five people on any time frame, and Boss wanted everything finished by the morning after our flight. By the following sunrise, we could move to a safe house that Ian had arranged for us and spend a few days recovering. But from the moment we arrived in Colorado, carrying out the attack against the Five Heads seemed far easier than the preparations themselves.

* * *

The moon shone brightly, exposing the flat strip of asphalt threading its way between steep hills. I leaned my head against the pickup, now parked in the middle of the road with the hood up. Karma was driving the other truck, which she had parked in a similar fashion a mile and a half down the road from me.

Boss, Matz, and Ophie worked between us, establishing their ambush site.

I crossed my arms tightly against my chest, trying to ward off a chill heightened by our elevation in the hills. The crisp night air seemed to crystallize the stars in stark clarity, their positions fixed amid a glaring lack of clouds in the midnight blue sky. That same tinge of frigidness had silenced almost all wildlife in the vicinity save the occasional call of an owl. Without the solemn chant of crickets, frogs, or other ambient noise, the ceaseless high-pitched ringing in my ears seemed as loud as ever. In any other setting, I would have begun drinking to lift my thoughts out of the darkness. Now, devoid of alcohol, I could only sit and wait for the sun to rise while letting my mind tear itself apart.

My cell phone vibrated, pulsing amidst the silence of the windless night.

I groaned and pulled the phone from my pocket. "Matz, I'm still fucking awake—"

A female voice responded, "He's been calling you, too?"

I sat up. "Hey, Karma. Yeah, I think he's afraid I'm passed out in the truck."

"I think he's afraid that I fucked off into town to get cigarettes."

"I'm surprised you haven't."

"I haven't run out of smokes yet. Why did you guys look like shit when I came to pick you up earlier today?"

"Probably because we'd just spent hours shuttling mortar equipment up the side of Mount Everest."

"Matz looked worse than any of you."

"He's been shot in the leg. Of course he looked worse than any of us."

"So why in God's name did you carry a sledgehammer up there?"

"To pound the baseplates down before we locked in the tubes. Otherwise, you have to fire a few rounds to get it to settle."

"I thought you looked very natural with it."

"I'll keep that in mind when we do the photo shoot for our team calendar."

"So what's it like to want to kill yourself?"

I sighed and turned my eyes skyward. "Diving right in to the intervention, are we?"

"Life is short, David." I heard the flicker of a lighter over the line.

"It's like being a teenager in Catholic school," I said. "Intense feelings of desire at all times, and the fact that everyone tells you it's wrong and you're going to hell doesn't stop your hormones. Whether or not you act on it is beside the point."

"Why don't you see a doctor?"

"I don't like pills."

"No, you don't like asking for help. I think you should consider medication."

"There's nothing drugs can do for you that alcohol can't."

"What if I wanted you to see a doctor? What if I went with you?"

"No, thanks."

"But you're attracted to me."

"I'm attracted to lots of women. That doesn't mean I take orders from them."

"It's more than that, though. Or am I wrong?"

"You're the only woman in a house full of guys, so there's not a lot of competition. Don't get carried away, Karma."

"I catch guys looking at me all the time. But I catch you trying desperately not to. Why would that be?"

"I'll do my best to objectify you more in the future."

"Why didn't you call me tonight?"

I rested my free hand against the grip of the Glock hidden under my jacket. "I'm bonding with nature."

"You could have called. We've been out here long enough."

"You know the reason."

"No, I don't."

"You're Matz's ex."

"Am I?"

"Which is fine. But there are lines I can't cross."

"You're an idiot."

"It's a guy thing, Karma. He's a complete prick, I'll give you that. But he's saved my life more than once, and in more than one way, and I'm not going to do that to him."

"I'm not his ex. I'm his sister."

I paused. "No wonder you're such a bitch."

"Is that better or worse than being his ex?"

"Infinitely worse."

"And how pathetic do you think I am to believe I'd date a guy like Matz?"

"Fair point. I'll apologize in person tomorrow."

"You'll apologize in person today. It's midnight."

I checked my watch. "So it is. Since we're being blunt, what are you doing here?"

"What do you mean?"

"You know what I mean. This work."

"We all have our motivations, David."

"Yes, but I can't figure out what yours are. You seem to hate everything we're doing."

She went silent, leaving me to the ringing in my ears.

"The first time Matz called me, I hadn't talked to him in years. It was a chance to see my brother again. Then, it became two driving gigs a year that paid for every expense I could possibly have."

"But you've continued doing it."

"I have to."

"Why?"

"Matz won't let me see him outside of this. And he wasn't the same after leaving the military. He's got issues from whatever he did over there, and he doesn't want to get help either."

"Having seen him in action, I'm not so sure he's bothered by it."

"Oh, you won't see it when he's in action. You'll see it when he isn't. He can't handle normalcy anymore."

"What about the others?"

"You want my amateur opinion?"

"I do."

"Boss is running away from something. His mind never stops working, so he has to keep it channeled. I don't think he gets any enjoyment from this work; it's a compulsive act for him. When his brain is consumed by planning missions, he's not thinking of his past."

"And Ophie?"

"He does it because he can. I don't think he gives a shit about anything. To him, this is slightly more fun than deer hunting."

"Who does that leave?"

"Us."

"What would you say about me?"

"You're too smart for your own good, but you do nothing with your intelligence besides wallow in self-loathing. You're the only person I've ever met who doesn't believe in God but still hates him. And you can resist sexual attraction, but will roll over in a heartbeat for a bottle of scotch."

"Bourbon."

"Bourbon," she corrected herself. "Other than that, how did I do?"

"Not bad."

"You're also straddling the line between being an adrenaline junkie and just having some kind of cliché death wish."

"Nice addition—not quite under the buzzer, Karma, but I'll accept it despite your glaring misunderstanding of my liquor proclivities. Normally I'd take extreme offense, so consider this a compliment."

"Your turn. What would you say about me, David?"

"I haven't really been paying attention. Give me a week."

"Tell me now," she said, the syllables spoken long and slow and likely with an indifferent exhale of cigarette smoke.

"You're kind by nature, and by extension nice to everyone you meet. Others are happy around you."

"Cut the shit, David. You sound like a fortune cookie."

I closed my eyes, picturing her expression as she awaited my response. "You are fucking gorgeous, think you know what's best for everyone else, and are mildly narcissistic. All three occasionally blur the line between well-intentioned commentary and condescending declarations on the nature of life and happiness that you project onto others."

"That doesn't mean I'm always wrong."

"No, but you've never been in a situation where you were about to die, or had to take someone else's life. You've also never looked inward to find yourself truly alone. As a result, you find it easy to judge those who have, which happens to include everyone on the road between us right now."

"Anything else?"

"You'd be a great mother because you already treat everyone like a child."

"Do I?"

"I think so."

"A little heavy-handed, but some fair points."

"Did I miss anything?"

"Yes."

"Such as?"

"I used to have a serious coke problem, and everything that went with it.

I'm a couple years older than you, and I've seen what recovery looks like, so don't think I'm being a hypocrite when I say you need help."

"I see."

"And Matz and I grew up with an abusive father."

"I'm sorry. How did Matz handle that?"

"Matz was seventeen when he put our father in the hospital. He just lost it. After that, it was the Army or jail. And I never got my brother back."

"Where is your dad now?"

"Where do you think?"

"Knowing Matz, I'm guessing he has since died of less than natural causes."

"You're very perceptive."

My phone beeped. "Shit, hang on. It's Matz."

"Wonderful."

I switched calls.

"You've reached David's phone. Please leave a message at the—"

"You awake?" Matz asked.

"More than ever. How's everything going out there?"

"The kill zone is set up and sectors of fire are clean. We've got the rockets and machine gun cached, but it'll take a few more hours to bury the charges."

"Oh." I paused. "Are you feeling better?"

"Fuck you."

"I just wanted to make sure you're okay, because earlier you looked a little—"

He hung up, and I switched lines.

"Okay, I'm back."

"Hi," she said.

"Hi."

"I'm running out of cigarettes."

"If it makes you feel better, I didn't have any in the first place."

"Too bad you're not here."

"Why, would you share with me?"

"Want to find out?"

"Sort of."

"Do you want to find out?"

"What do you think, Karma?"

"I want to hear it from you."

"Then ask me in person."

A few seconds passed before she said, "What was the name of the girl you were supposed to marry, the one who slept with your best friend?"

"Sarah."

"And the girl after her?"

"Laila."

"Tell me about Laila's ex."

I rolled my shoulder blades, feeling my back pop, before relaxing again. "She left him for me. He didn't handle it well. I called to get him to leave her alone. He called me back once after that. Words were exchanged both times."

"And what was your very rational response to this dick-measuring contest?"

"I blew his fucking head off."

"You did that for her?"

"I did that for myself."

"Would you kill someone for me?"

"If that's what you wanted me to do for you."

"Are there other options?"

"You'll have to ask me in person, Karma."

I heard her exhale smoke into the phone. "Maybe I will."

* * *

The safe house was a modest, residential structure surrounded by trees and positioned between two neighborhoods. Although we had been awake for more than twenty-four hours, Matz and Ophie sprang to life as soon as we pulled into the driveway. They leapt from the truck, grabbed their bags, and ran up the walkway to the front steps—Ophie tripping Matz on the way—before unlocking the door. The second Ophie swung it open, Matz elbowed him out of the doorway and ran inside first.

"Children," Karma muttered as Boss and I stepped out of the truck. She took out her suitcase and calmly carried it to the house, leaving Boss and me to unload the remaining bags. By then, our gear only consisted of personal belongings and everyone's individual weapons except for mine; my M4 and Glock had been staged at the mortar position and were awaiting my arrival.

By the time Boss and I walked through the door, Ophie and Matz had already run through the house and declared ownership of their bedrooms. Matz, now satisfied, walked to the bathroom with a towel slung over his shoulder.

He checked the handle, but found it locked. On the other side of the door, we heard the shower turn on.

"No, no, no," Matz called. "I've got first shower! You take forever."

Karma replied through the door, "This happened when you two fought over the best bedroom in the last safe house. Remember?"

"No, it didn't."

"Yes, it did."

Ophie said, "She's right. I remember that now."

Matz shook his head and murmured, "Son of a bitch." Then, he composed himself and yelled, "I'll just kick down the fucking door."

"I'm naked," Karma reminded him.

"Then *I'll* kick down the fucking door," Ophie shouted. He started to run forward, but Matz threw him into the wall. Ophie tackled Matz around the ribs, and they crashed to the floor, each wrestling for the dominant position. I stepped over them and walked down the hallway to the kitchen, opening cabinets until I found one filled with half-empty bottles. Rummaging through them, I selected a handle of Jim Beam and turned to see Boss standing behind me.

He said, "If you need a sleep aid right now, you're beyond all hope."

I studied the bottle. "I find the medicinal and restorative properties of alcohol somewhat rejuvenating after a long night awake."

"So do I." Boss opened the fridge and peered inside. He withdrew a bottle of beer, examining the label with a nod of approval. "Ian's been finding my favorite IPA for years now, no matter where we travel. Next time, we'll ask him to stock a bottle of your bourbon."

"I thought there wasn't going to be a next time," I said, finding a glass.

Boss's face showed the faint trace of a smile as he popped open his beer with a bottle opener he found on the counter. He seated himself at the round table, leaving me to fish some ice cubes out of the freezer before filling my glass with amber liquid. I sat down across from him.

He held his beer bottle toward me, and I clinked my glass against it.

"You're going to miss this, aren't you?"

He shrugged. "A few years ago, this kind of work didn't exist. Soon, it will never exist again. You're coming in at the end of the gold rush. The war between these organizations wasn't going to last forever."

"What type of organizations are they?"

He took a sip of beer and set down the bottle.

"The less you know, the better."

"I think I'm starting to prove myself to you."

"You've absolutely proven yourself to me. That's why I'm telling you that the less you know, the better."

"Is the Handler as evil as Ian says?"

"Ian's not an action guy, David. He's the guy who sits in front of computers and radios and tells us what we need to know, but he's never put a bullet through anything in his life, except a paper target. Everything's scary to him. That's why you have us."

"I'm not asking about Ian."

"You think the Handler doesn't bleed? We could get to him, too, if we took the time. But if any of us survived the effort, it wouldn't be for long."

"How do you think this next job is going to turn out?"

"Not well."

"Why do you say that?"

He sat back in his chair. "We've never done anything like this before. They won't see it coming."

"Then why do you say 'not well?'"

"You wouldn't believe me if I told you."

"Try me."

"All right. I had a dream right before Caspian got killed. Actually, I've had that same dream with startling regularity every time I've lost someone, both during my time in the military and afterward."

"And you're having it again?"

"It's different this time."

"How?"

He shook his head slightly. "One of us is going to die on the next mission, and this time I think it's going to be me."

"What does the dream involve?"

"A ship."

"What else?"

He shook his head again. "That stays between us, you understand?"

"Why are you telling me and not the others?"

"Because you're not going to turn into the others, David. You're going to turn into me."

A door slammed in the house, startling us. He sighed and settled his shoulders. I leaned forward in my seat, taking a long pull of whiskey as we heard the shower start again.

Boss continued, "The worst enemy those guys will ever face is a man with a gun. Ours is our own mind, and you can't kill that unless you do it for good. Other than that, the only difference between you and me is about twenty years of experience and your alcohol tolerance."

"That sounds like a compliment."

"It's not. You're an arrogant little cocksucker, but so was I. You're a quick study, and the guys are giving you shit while they can. If this business is around for you to stay in, you'd be giving the orders someday. So be careful when you decide what you're going to do after our last job. Because this"— he held out his arms, his beer bottle in one hand, his exhausted eyes leveling with mine—"is what the view looks like."

* * *

The house was silent as I emerged from the bathroom, feeling clean but disagreeably sober. I put my bag and towel in my bedroom, the last one to remain after the others staked their claim. I returned to the kitchen and poured a tall drink over ice, then raised it to my face to smell its cool, comforting vapors. Before long, I was wrapped in that familiar, sweet warmth that absorbed me into its safety, the lover's embrace that calmed my racing mind and pulsing body. My thoughts slowed back down to a harmonious vibration as I set down the glass, now empty aside from a few lonely ice cubes.

I returned to my room to get some sleep while the requisite amount of alcohol took hold in my system. Shutting the door, I stripped to a pair of gym shorts and lay down beneath the blanket, my mind spinning pleasantly as I closed my eyes. When my thoughts were laced with liquor, I experienced no jaw-clenching ruminations on the past, no thoughts of where I went wrong or what mistakes I made, no rubbing my temples and staring at the floor, exhaling endlessly. Alcohol was certainly an evil, but it was much less of an evil than the alternative, and it allowed me to buffer myself from the reality of my life, and of my past, at will.

The high-frequency ringing in both ears likewise ranged from a harsh inconvenience to a barely noticeable detail, depending on the number of drinks in my system. Although it wasn't bothering me at the moment, my hearing was still damaged. I never heard my bedroom door creak open, but I did hear it close.

My eyes opened to see Karma standing in front of me, her hair pulled back in a wet ponytail. She was wearing a pair of cotton shorts and a T-shirt with no bra, and she approached my bed silently. Then she pulled back my blanket and straddled my waist. The mattress creaked as she lowered her face to mine.

I whispered, "Your brother is right next door."

She put her lips against my ear. "Life is short, David." Her weight shifted as she rubbed her thighs against me. "I want you to see a doctor."

"I'm not going to."

"It feels like you're considering it."

She kissed my neck, and then sat up. Her hands caressed her stomach before she held the bottom of her T-shirt and slowly pulled it off. My eyes roamed her body, taking in the tattoos I hadn't yet seen. She reached behind her head with both hands, rolling her hips in a circular motion as she let her hair down around her shoulders.

I put my hands on her thighs and slid them upwards to her hips. She took my wrists and pinned them over my head, lowering herself over me to whisper in my ear again, "I want you to see a doctor."

"I think that's an excellent idea."

"I'm going with you."

"Okay."

"Promise me."

"I promise."

She resumed kissing my neck as she rubbed her body back and forth over mine. "What was your fiancée's name?"

"You know, I have no idea."

She kissed my chest. "Who was your last girlfriend?"

"I don't remember."

She trailed her lips up my neck to my chin, stopping just short of my mouth. Then she wrapped her palm around my jaw, squeezing my cheeks in her hand. Her face hovered over mine, her lucid blue eyes staring at me.

"And who am I, David?"

"Karma."

She leaned forward, letting her breasts graze my face before bringing her eyes back to mine. "Say it again."

"Karma."

She smiled and brought her lips to my ear. "After this, you're going to remember me for the rest of your fucking life."

And I did.

17

"Suicide!" Matz yelled. "Get your fucking ass over here and sit down."

I turned from the cabinet, and he saw the whiskey bottle in my hands. His face darkened with angry disbelief as he addressed me very slowly, as if speaking to a child.

"Put that back right now. Boss picked out a few nice bottles of Cabernet, and you're not pairing whiskey with my fettuccine with tomato, pancetta, and chèvre."

Karma, seated across the table from Matz, turned around in her chair and glared at me.

"He's been cooking all day, David. Show a little respect."

I put the bottle back.

The sole remaining seat at the table faced Boss, and as I took it he and I sat in the same chairs we had the first time we spoke in the safe house. Karma had painstakingly set the table, arranging three candles around bowls of salad and pasta, a salt shaker that went untouched, a basket of bread, and several bottles of wine, one of which Ophie was working to uncork.

He handed the open bottle to Boss, and we watched in silence as Boss poured a generous portion of wine into each glass. He looked over every face at the table before saying, "Before commencing our final team dinner in America, I would like to summon Reverend Ophie to deliver the invocation."

Ophie, who had been examining his fingernails, looked up before clearing his throat. "Shit, it's... ah, it's been a while since I've done one of these. I'll try to dust off the cobwebs... Let us join hands."

Matz extended his palm and looked at me expectantly. I glanced around the table, noting that the others had joined hands already.

Sighing with resignation, I took Matz's hand with my left and Karma's with my right.

Ophie closed his eyes and bowed his head.

"Merciful and loving Father, we gather here tonight in thanksgiving for the food and fellowship you have so graciously bestowed upon us. Dear Lord, we know this is a stupid fucking plan, what with David slingshotting across the sky to his death in a squirrel suit and a three-man ambush team with me as its only warrior... since Matz has been filled with too many bullets and is nearly a gimp and Boss is so old he went to fucking middle school with your Son."

Karma shouted, "Preach it, brother, preach it!"

"But in your infinite wisdom and tenderness, give us the steely eyes to stare the devil in the face one last time, the steady hands to detonate high explosives and incinerate our enemy before slinging rockets and lead into any survivors trying to run out of the wreckage because they're on goddamn fire, the strong hearts to flee the scene on foot and make it to our getaway cars before security or law enforcement arrive and have to get shot in the fucking face, too, because they're standing in the way of us and our retirement fund."

Matz's eyes were pinched shut in concentration as he yelled, "Hallelujah! Hosanna!"

"And, finally, wise and graceful Father, look over us poor bastards at our final destination. In your heavenly light, may you protect us from the venereal scourges of model-tier prostitutes, from the sinful brutality of mamajuana hangovers, and from letting Boss smoke so much weed that he actually relaxes for the first time in his very, very long life. Amen."

Everyone released hands and applauded politely.

Ophie turned his eyes skyward before adding, "That's the product of eight years of good, wholesome Baptist schooling right there. I told you those tuition checks wouldn't go to waste, Momma. Miss you every day."

* * *

I never saw Boss touch his glass of wine, though nobody else seemed to notice.

The others had no such problem; by now, the dishes had long been cleared and Ophie was opening the third bottle while toying with Matz, who was seated across from him.

"And what, exactly, are you going to do with this car once you get it? Nothing but dirt roads down there, anyway."

"Bullshit," Matz replied. "There are plenty of Ferraris there already; I'll just be importing the first F40."

Beside me, Karma rolled her eyes. "That car is not going to solve your problems."

"Yes, it will," Matz and Ophie responded in unison.

Boss leaned forward and placed his palm flat on the table, silencing the group. Looking at the wall behind me, he said, "I'm tired, guys. I need to prepare for what's ahead."

"You never sleep," Matz replied.

"I will this time."

Ophie said, "Get your old ass to bed, then."

Boss rose slowly from his chair. "Goodnight, gentlemen. Karma."

As he turned and walked out of the dining room, Ophie looked back at Matz. "You won't even be able to get one into the country."

Matz resolutely shook his head. "You're severely underestimating this place, man. I won't even have to pay import tax, because you can bribe a politician for the exemption. And the money launderers can get anything they want in and out of the ports."

As I looked at the dark doorway that Boss had passed through, Karma's hand touched my knee under the table and began tracing the curve of my thigh. Sliding my eyes to her, I saw that her face was directed toward the others.

"Excuse me," I said, standing to leave.

Matz said, "You're not going to bed already, are you? You and I still have something we need to talk about."

"No, I'll be right back."

I rounded the corner into the hallway and headed for the bathroom before stopping and looking over my shoulder. I could hear Karma's voice over the clank of bottle against glass, followed by Ophie's raucous laughter.

Turning, I continued down the hall to Boss's room.

His door was closed, and I gave it two light raps with my knuckle. No response. I turned the handle and opened the door to see Boss sitting on the corner of his bed in the lit room, leaning forward with his elbows on his knees. He was staring at a single photograph in his hands, and I caught a glimpse of smiling twin girls before he looked up at me with tears in his eyes and a weary face that bore the pain of a lifetime.

"David," he said quietly, "I knew you'd come."

"I just wanted to see how you were doing."

"Looking for the profound last words of your team leader?"

"Something like that."

He smirked and turned his eyes back to the photograph. "Then here they are: everything we do—all the guns, the money, the planning, all of it —is just a distraction to keep us occupied from our own realities. If you live your life right, you won't need any of that."

"What about everything you said to me that first night in the basement, about flirting—"

"Flirting with death? The perfect rush? We needed you to kill Saamir for us, and we needed it done on a timeline. If you weren't as fucked in the head as I am, I would have just offered you cash and been done with it. And I'm telling you the truth now, because I won't get another chance after you leave that plane tomorrow."

"A dream can't predict the future, Boss."

"Ian's going to get you guys down south. I'm not worried about that. But once you get there, take care of Matz and Ophie. They went through a lot well before you joined us, so get them whatever they need. Listen to Karma in that regard, because when it comes down to it, she knows those two better than they know themselves."

"I'll take care of all three of them, Boss. You have my word. I don't want you to worry about that now."

"After that, my final wish for you is that you take your share and start over. Get married, have a family, and put everything you've done with us in that place inside that your wife won't know about, along with everything you've already got from Afghanistan and Iraq. Veterans have been doing that since the dawn of war, and now it's your turn."

"You're really sure you'll die out there?"

"David, I've never been more certain of anything in my entire life. This one will be it for me, and I'm going into it with my eyes open. Now let me be."

"Goodnight, Boss. And thank you for everything."

"Goodnight, David."

I backed out of the room and into the hallway, gently closing the door before walking back to join the others.

* * *

When I returned to my seat at the table, I saw Matz looking at Karma.

"All right," he said, "time to go. The adults have to talk."

Karma replied, "Since I'm not trustworthy enough yet?"

"There are things you don't need to know."

I felt her hand on my thigh again, but she never took her eyes off Matz as she slid it upward. "You realize I'm the only one in this house who really likes you, right?"

"It's not a popularity contest."

"Lucky for you." She began moving her hand back and forth on my lap. "You may want to think twice before pissing me off, Matz."

"Leave us."

"Sure thing. Have a great night, everyone. I know I will." She gave my pants a final, firm rub before tilting back her head to drink the last of her wine. She stood, pushed in her chair, and left.

Ophie sat back, neatly folding his hands across his abdomen. "And then there were three. Nice work, Matz. Let's upset David's getaway driver."

Undeterred, Matz leaned forward, his intense eyes staring into mine. "You know how bad we need those mortars, right?"

"Sure," I said, shifting in my seat. "They'll trigger the entire operation."

"I'm not talking about that. I'm talking about the whole thing. Years of work leading up to this retirement. There were six of us when we started—"

"Matz," Ophie said, "take it easy on the poor kid. He's got enough to prepare for tomorrow."

"He's the single point of failure. He needs to hear it."

"Fuck, Matz." Ophie pushed back his chair and stood. "Whatever. I'm not sticking around for this."

He left, and Matz and I were alone.

Matz continued, "There were six of us when we started, and Ophie wasn't one of them. Boss and I were there from the beginning, and so were four others who died along the way. Caspian was just the last to get killed. There were a few new recruits who didn't make it this far, either. This is bigger than all of us, and I don't think you really understand that because we've kept so much from you."

"And why would that be, Matz? I think I've done enough to earn my keep so far."

"Don't get any delusions of grandeur, you little shit. You don't know a fucking thing about what this team has done since the beginning, and we haven't told you because you're the most expendable. Who do you think is the most likely to get captured alive before this is over? The three of us on the ambush, or you out there by yourself?"

"I'm not getting captured alive."

"You better not. I don't really care if you make it out, but you need to do your job out there. We've done dozens of missions against this organization, and now the leadership will be in one place, for one meeting, before we can disband the team and retire. None of that means fuck-all if you don't fire those mortars on time, and me and Boss and Ophie haven't gone through what we have in the past few years to watch you fuck it up. Do it if it kills you, you understand me? The survivors from this team deserve to retire in peace."

"Matz, I think I've got a solution for all your concerns."

"And what's that?"

"Since you're so worried about the mortars, why don't you shoot them? I'll gladly take your place on the ambush line. You go ahead and freefall out of a plane at sunset tomorrow—and figure out my wingsuit and BASE rig on the way down—then land your parachute on that postage stamp of a landing area without dying. Let me know how that works out for you."

Matz's face settled into a stony stare as I continued, "Until then, don't tell me how to do my fucking job. I'm willing to die for this team just as much as you, Boss, or Ophie are. I don't need any reminders from you that I'm the new guy, because no one else seems to have a problem with it."

"Just don't fuck it up, Suicide."

"I won't, Matz."

He scraped back his chair, then rose stiffly and moved toward the hall.

I called after him, "Dinner was excellent, by the way."

He continued walking away as he replied, "I know my pancetta is fucking gangster. I don't need to hear it from you."

He vanished down the hall, and I poured myself another serving of wine from the last remaining bottle.

* * *

Ophie strolled back into the dining room before I'd finished my glass.

He glanced into the kitchen before asking, "Did our resident asshole finally turn in for the night?"

"Yes."

"Thank God." Ophie pulled his chair back out, then poured himself another glass and raised it in the air to toast me. I mirrored the gesture, and together we took a sip.

I set down my glass and said, "Why did you get so upset over Matz giving me his little pep talk?"

Ophie shook his head, observing my expression with amusement. "You're a big boy—you can handle Matz. I just needed an excuse to leave."

"For what?"

He gave a sidelong glance over his shoulder and listened for a moment before reaching into his pocket. He pulled out a thin silver spike and slid it across the table toward me.

I reached out to grab it, holding it up to my face and turning it over in the light.

"Is this the firing pin for a Glock?" I asked, sliding it back to him.

He caught it and grinned. "Good eye, David."

"Whose is it?"

"Whose do you think?"

I frowned, meeting Ophie's level stare. "Matz isn't going to do anything stupid. He's already talking about getting his car."

"His leg's injured, David, and he's not going to let himself slow us down if he can't keep up after the ambush."

"I don't think Matz would do that."

"You know, for someone who gives you so much shit for almost killing yourself, I think the same thought has crossed his mind a few times. I've found him before, just sitting on that back porch facing the range where we used to stuff you in that goddamn box. Just sitting there with a pistol in his hand, staring at the woods."

"He's been to combat. Who knows what goes through his head."

"I've seen flashbacks, and that wasn't it. There are things worse than war, David. And for the type of man who has seen those things, combat can become a respite."

I took another drink, rotating my hand to look at the glass. "You think anyone's going to die on this one?"

"From our side?" He shrugged. "I can tell you one thing: if anybody bites it out there, it ain't going to be me."

"I don't think God's going to protect you after your dinner sermon."

He smirked. "Hell, a few missions ago we were on the objective for about ten minutes flat, and it was one of those days where I came inches from death a few times. Later, when we were driving to meet Joe at the airport, we saw a minivan that had rolled over and was surrounded by cop cars. The family was already in body bags. Happened on a straight stretch of road with another car wrecked off to the side. Who knows what the fuck happened. Why'd they die and I survive? Because I deserved it and they didn't?"

"Why do you think?"

"Because God doesn't care about us. It's all random and meaningless, boy, and I think you know that much by now."

I released a weary sigh. "Maybe you're right."

"I am right. You know, I started my career being certain I'd get killed. After enough missions, I started to think maybe I'd make it. And by now, I know I'm going to die of natural causes."

"Not a bad way to go."

"Eh, it's so-so. It kind of takes the fun out of things—half the thrill of combat is not knowing if you're going to get killed or not, right?"

I watched his expression, trying to ascertain if he was serious or not. "So why'd you use a .22 to kill Peter?" he asked. "You had a bear gun for yourself, but hit him with a peashooter. I never asked you why."

I grinned sheepishly, my eyes dropping to the table. "To be honest, Ophie, I... I wanted him to survive long enough to talk a little bit. I wanted to see what he had to say when he met me."

Ophie smiled at this, absentmindedly observing the contents of his glass as he swirled it. Then he stopped abruptly, swallowed the rest, and said, "Well, better get some sleep before the big day. You're the star of the show tomorrow, David."

He rose without waiting for a response. I sat alone, listening to his footsteps moving down the hall. After finishing my glass, I went to my room, swung the door open, and closed it again with a bang.

Then I went to Karma's room and slid inside, gingerly easing her door shut behind me.

PROMISED LAND

Post tenebras lux

-After the darkness, light

18

I pulled up the sliding cargo door and cold wind spilled inside, roaring above the sound of the plane's engine. I set my left hand, bearing a luminescent altimeter, on the bottom edge of the exit door and my other hand against the lead corner, then settled my knees on the aircraft floor and leaned my head outside.

The blast of air pushed my clear wraparound goggles tight against my face, whipping my hair into disarray as I watched the wrinkled landscape easing by fourteen thousand feet below us. The ground was bathed in the neon orange of oncoming dusk, and the irregular outline of the approaching lake resembled a loosely coiled serpent; the final rays of sun beamed off its spiked tail, which pointed almost directly toward my landing area 2.8 kilometers away.

Sticking my head back inside, I saw Matz feigning disinterest on the seat across from me. Karma looked at me with concern, and Ophie, beside her, tilted his head to hear me.

"Five left!" I called to Ophie.

Ophie yelled toward the cockpit, "Five degrees left!"

I stuck my head back outside the plane, watching our line of flight adjust slightly toward the crease in the shoreline that I had chosen as my exit point.

For the majority of the flight, I had been staring out a right side window, tracking the roads, lakes, and hills leading up to a tiny landing area that I wouldn't be able to see until seconds before deploying my parachute. As we neared the lake, my only focus was ensuring that our line of flight remained perfectly aligned with the left shoreline—aside from our altitude, my exit point was the only factor I could control in advance. Once I jumped, everything depended on my reflexes and being able to maintain my body position to fly the wingsuit beneath my BASE rig.

Pulling my head back into the plane, I rose to a crouched position and shuffled toward the cockpit, catching high-fives from Karma and Ophie along the way. As I approached the front, Boss looked at me from his position in the copilot seat.

"We're all counting on you, David, and I know you're going to deliver. Fire those mortars on time, no matter what."

I set a hand on his shoulder. "I'm not letting you down, Boss—not my style. Joe, this heading is perfect."

Joe looked over from the controls. "I'll hold it here. You've got about thirty seconds to the lake."

"Nice flying with you again." I squeezed Boss's shoulder. "I'll see you tomorrow at the linkup. You'll see."

He nodded to me, but said nothing.

I turned back to the cabin and moved toward the cargo door, yelling, "Matz! Boss needs you up front. Now."

Matz hurried to his feet and slid around me, approaching the cockpit with his head bowed. Stepping around Ophie, I stopped in front of Karma, who was watching me intently. I lifted my hands as much as the wings of my suit allowed and pulled her face toward mine. I kissed her lips for one second, then two, before pulling back to look at her.

She said, "Be careful out there, David. Promise me."

"It's okay, I'm fucking immortal."

At that moment, I heard Matz scream from the cockpit, high above the roar of the wind and the engine, "WHAT THE FUCK!"

I kissed Karma one last time, turned, and flung myself through the open door and into the blue abyss.

The buzz of the plane's engine faded as the howling sky filled my ears like crashing waves. The wind tumbled my body as I fell, keeping my arms to my sides and my legs pressed together. As soon as I cleared the plane's tail, I spread my limbs and felt the curved fabric cells of the arm and leg wings pressurize into a flying surface. I established stability and dipped my shoulder to bank in a right turn. Following the finger of the lake with my eyes as the wind pressed against my face, I picked up horizontal speed in the wingsuit as the ocean howl of the sky quieted to a whistling stream.

Once I was aimed in the right direction, I focused on adjusting my body position for optimum flight. My legs were locked straight out with toes pointed, and I rolled my shoulders forward to tweak the position of my arm wings. Slight bend downward at the waist, chin tucked to chest, and as soon as I ran through my mental checklist, I heard myself hitting the sweet spot of wingsuit flight, where the wind quiets and you can feel yourself surging forward at the best efficiency. Then, the sky became so quiet I could have talked to someone flying next to me.

I slid my chin sideways to sneak a glance at my altimeter, then peeked up toward the landing area. I was at nine thousand feet and gaining distance at a good pace. My eyes ticked off the landmarks beneath me and verified my heading. There was a particular hilltop that I wanted to pass over at five thousand feet, and I skimmed past it at 5,400.

As I soared over a small lake at 2,500 feet, my mind began screaming an alarm: I was passing through the hard deck of skydiving. I coasted through 1,500 feet, then passed a dirt road just shy of my landing area. I forced myself to hold my position, knowing the tiny field would be approaching in seconds. Then I tucked my hands to my sides, braced my knees and ankles together, arched my pelvis, and transitioned from flying to falling like a hawk diving out of the sky.

My right hand was clutching my pilot chute as I held this precarious position, trying to remain symmetrical and avoid rolling to one side or the other. I gauged when I was five hundred feet from impact, then pitched my pilot chute with my right hand before bringing my palms back to my chest.

I didn't have to wait in that position for long.

As my eyes absorbed the treetops slicing toward me at a vertical angle, an explosive *CRACK* flung my legs up in front of my face. The opening was so sudden and violent that for a moment I was afraid I would flip backwards through my risers, and certain that I would then look up to see my parachute in shreds. I threw my eyes skyward; the canopy was fully pressurized and flying cleanly and crisply as the wind blew softly against my face. I unzipped the sleeves of my wingsuit to free my arms for steering and crossed my ankles to collapse the leg wing as treetops approached at chest level.

Piloting my canopy left, I passed between the spiky tops of two pine trees; the side of my parachute scraped against loose sprigs as I drifted downward into waves of long grass. A pink haze from the dwindling sun glanced between sharp shadows beneath me and I pumped my hands gradually downward to flare. My canopy leveled into straight flight, then went nose up and stalled when my boots were two feet off the ground. Then I touched down so softly that I could have landed on one foot.

Turning to pull my parachute to the ground, I quickly looped the lines around one hand and threw them into the collapsing fabric, then balled that into a two-arm bundle before shuffling into the woods and out of sight. Once I had passed into the trees, I dropped the mass onto the mossy rocks at my feet. The thick, earthy forest air seemed overpowering after the scentless open wind of my flight. I sat to strip off the wingsuit and BASE harness. Stuffing everything into my stash bag, I cinched it shut and threw it onto my back, and then began moving toward the mortar firing point with what little daylight remained.

* * *

The night was black, with flickers of lightning from a turbulent sky illuminating the scene for split seconds at a time. Ocean waves crested violently, tossing a single ship in their wake, its masts sheared off and its sails in tatters. It pitched downward from the top of a wave and plunged toward the trough before everything went black. At the next flash of lightning, the ship was tipped upward once again, rising on the next wave. People clung to the deck as the sea flung the ship, now approaching a near vertical angle and beginning to skew sideways, before the lightning vanished and plunged the scene into blackness—

I burst awake to the sound of birdcalls and blinked at sunlight filtering through the treetops.

After unzipping my sleeping bag, I put on my boots and rose to begin the day's work. Strapping on body armor and my Glock, I slung my M4 with suppressor and conducted a short patrol around the hilltop, peering down the slopes to ensure I was alone.

My surroundings were far more beautiful that morning than they had been days prior, when we had parked the two pickups on a desolate spot on the dirt road now far below me. Our stopping point was surrounded by a labyrinthine forest, and the ground dropped off to the left, the wooded face of the earth molded in a steep descent hundreds of feet to the growl of a narrow river. The hill to the right rose sharply and was far more concerning.

I hadn't been able to appreciate the view from the top the first time I saw it, nor on successive trips spent shuttling mortar equipment and ammunition uphill that day as Ophie set up the firing point and dialed in the systems. But the scenery was unrivaled when I wasn't fatigued, and my mind drifted back to my wingsuit flight over the gloriously mottled sunset terrain and crystal bodies of water pooled amid foothills.

The view that morning was liberating in the crystalline sense of its beauty; it was reflective of the freedom I had experienced in the Smoky Mountains as a teenager. There was a certain tranquility to the majesty of nature that I could experience nowhere else, which captivated me regardless of my past or future. Before near-death experiences in combat and BASE jumping, before medicating myself with alcohol, and before memories of hiking with my best friend were tainted by his affair with my fiancée, those mountains had provided the greatest sense of freedom I had ever known.

After my patrol, I began uncovering the three mortars, removing first the camouflage netting that concealed them and then the tarps that waterproofed the systems. They were spaced a few feet apart, arrayed in descending order of height. The 120mm mortar was massive, its cannon standing as tall as a man. Together with its baseplate and bipod, the system weighed over three hundred pounds. The 81mm was slightly smaller, and the 60mm, with a cannon measuring less than four feet, looked like a miniature of both.

The effect of all three mortars shooting in succession would terrify those on the objective: a rhythmic sequence of distant *thumps* would sound over the hills, instantly recognizable to the war veterans among the security force. A brief period of abject disbelief and horror would lead to the first panicked cry to take cover, which would surely occur at some point in the fleeting thirty-eight seconds of flight time before the first mortar round impacted. The instant it did so, destroying everything at its point of impact and flinging shrapnel in a seventy-five meter radius, half a dozen more would be sailing through the air behind it.

Once the mortars were uncovered, I repeated the process with the ammo crates staged at the edge of the clearing and began laying out rounds. Whereas the 120mm rounds were monstrous and required two hands to hoist, the 60mm were toys by contrast. I laid them in neat rows by their respective mortar tubes, the rounds appearing as metal footballs with a length of tail emerging from the back and ringed with fins.

I consolidated my wingsuit, parachute, and sleeping gear in a heap behind the center mortar and recovered the overstuffed yellow hiking pack we had cached. Setting it on top of the pile, I opened the flap to see the enormous explosive charge that Matz had constructed and gave an involuntary whistle of awe. I unrolled a section of cord ending in two fuse igniters, setting it outside the pack for easy access. Matz had admittedly assembled the charge to the point of overkill; when I asked if I would be killed in the ensuing blast, he shrugged and said, "You've got one minute, plus or minus three seconds. It depends on how fast you run."

After conducting another patrol around the hillside to ensure no one was approaching, I transmitted to Ian.

"Red, this is White. I send Coin Toss and request confirmation of Kickoff."

"White, Red. Copy Coin Toss. No change to kickoff time."

"Copy." I checked my watch, synchronized by Boss before I left, and saw I had eighteen minutes to go. No change to the plan meant that Boss, Matz, and Ophie must have completed their ground movement and were already stationed at the ambush site.

Carrying my rifle at the ready, I performed a final, circular patrol around the hilltop, peering down the forested slope in all directions. Light from the rising sun trickled through the leaves, and I felt its warmth wash over me amid the sound of birdcalls. When five minutes remained on my countdown, I transmitted to Ian.

"Red, this is White. Request confirmation of Kickoff."

"*White, Red. No change.*"

"Copy."

I watched the clock tick down, agonizingly slow in its progress. At one minute out, I tightened the sling of my M4 to keep it out of my way while firing and picked up a set of shooting earmuffs. Although my radio earpieces doubled as hearing protection, the mortars were loud enough to warrant extra insurance to preserve whatever hearing I had left.

A moment before I positioned the muffs over my ears, I heard the snap of a branch down the hill to my front.

I froze.

Slowly, I lowered the hearing protection away from my head. Setting the muffs on the ground, I loosened my M4 sling and readied the rifle as I walked to a tree at the end of the clearing. I took cover behind its trunk and eased my rifle around the side to scan the downhill slope. At first, I saw nothing except for the dense greenery I had already surveyed during my short patrols. Then, I heard another branch break to my left. I aimed my M4 toward the sound, focusing my vision down the hill and hoping against all odds that I would only find a deer.

Instead, a man walked diagonally up the slope a hundred meters below me. He was dressed in civilian camouflage, and at a slightly greater distance could have passed for a hunter. But he carried a black assault rifle that I couldn't identify and wore a vest like mine that surely held ammunition and a radio. His head turned to the side intermittently, and it became clear to me that he was having a quiet conversation just before I saw the second man.

The men appeared to be on a routine security patrol, conducting gradual switchbacks up the hillside toward me. I could tell they didn't expect anyone to be on top of the mountain. They weren't maneuvering tactically, although that would surely change once I fired the first mortar round. I heard another noise and glimpsed a third man through the trees, walking in front of the other two. The terrain was on my side; they would have a steep uphill fight to overrun me.

But that was my lone advantage.

I didn't know how many were among them or their number of rein-forcements, and firing the mortars would leave me completely vulnerable to their assault. Leveling my sights on their party, I watched them pass in and out of view through my optic as they moved between the trees. By now, they were perhaps eighty meters away from me. I couldn't tell who was in charge, and absent that knowledge tried to get a bead on the lead man to discourage their advance. He vanished behind the trees, and I moved my sights to chest level along his path, waiting for him to emerge. He reap-peared a few steps later, walking forward into the aim of my suppressed M4.

At that moment, my watch alarm began beeping. He looked uphill and directly at me.

I fired two well-aimed shots, chasing them with five more in rapid succession. He dropped out of sight. I swung my rifle to the left, spreading another ten bullets back and forth where I suspected the other two men stood. I heard them yelling to each other. Rifle fire cracked to my right, and I turned to see muzzle flashes from a second group of men located fifty meters from the security patrol I'd just shot at. I returned fire until I had expended my magazine. By then, the first group had also begun shooting.

I turned and ran to the mortars, pulling the sling so my M4 was tight against my side. I hoisted the first 120mm round off the ground and slid the tail into the tube until my hands reached the rim.

I released my hands from the round and swept them down the outside of the cannon, feeling the concussion of the mortar system roaring to life with a massive explosion as the round rocketed upward into the sky. Grabbing the next round off the ground, I repeated the process as quickly as I could. The *BOOM* of the mortar repeated at a cadence as I fell into the routine, wanting to get all seven of the 120mm rounds downrange to flush our targets toward the ambush. I knew the men on the hill would hesitate at the initial blast but recognize the rhythmic explosions in seconds.

Once they did, they would launch their assault; as long as that mortar continued to shoot, the men they were being paid to protect would die.

As the final 120mm round blasted off, I ran to the tree line while reloading my rifle. Ducking behind a tree trunk, I angled out to aim at the source of sporadic gunfire coming at me from the right side. As I began sweeping the firing positions with bullets, gunshots erupted from the team on my left—they were now only fifty meters away, having closed the distance while the other team provided covering fire.

Bullets hissed over my head and cracked into the tree in front of me. I emptied the rest of my magazine at the men, then ran back to the mortars. I heard the distant *crunk* of the first rounds impacting at their destination, and I skidded to a halt in front of the 81mm rounds. I was able to load these lighter rounds into the tube more quickly, and I fired the first five before moving back to the woods. After reloading my rifle on the move, I looked up to see a thick haze of violet mist rising up from twenty-five meters below me.

The men were using smoke grenades to conceal their maneuver, and were now closing in too fast for me to stop them. Gunfire continued from the other side of the hill, the bullets zipping through the trees at a steady rate.

If I ran to the tree line again, I'd be shot.

I stopped in place, then threw one grenade to the left and one to the right. The trees below me were too dense for accurate aim, but the explosions would cause the men to reevaluate how badly they wanted to overrun that hilltop. Running back to the mortars, I bypassed the 81mm and moved to the hiking pack, grasping the two igniters with my left hand and activating them with my right by giving each ring a quarter turn before pulling it up toward me.

I fired the remaining 81mm rounds as quickly as I could, my arms beginning to tire by the time I lifted the tenth and final one. Gunfire from the hillside to my front continued, and I saw more violet smoke rising ten meters into the woods. I hurled another two grenades in separate directions and transitioned to the last mortar before they exploded. I heard the impact of the 81mm rounds resonating through the hills amid the security team's rifle bursts, and picked up the first 60mm round as my grenades detonated.

I knelt next to the tube, dropping the rounds in one after another as the small cannon bucked with each shot.

An explosion burst in the clearing ahead of me, raining dirt over my head. At first, I thought a mortar round had misfired and landed short before realizing that I was receiving incoming grenades from the men assaulting the hilltop.

I was being overrun.

Throwing a final grenade, I dropped another two 60mm rounds down the tube. A second incoming grenade exploded, the concussion knocking me down. Gasping for breath with my head ringing, I felt a tiny shred of hot shrapnel smoldering in the right side of my neck. Struggling to my hands and knees, I realized the piece of metal had missed my artery by perhaps half an inch. At that point, I had no idea how many 60mm rounds remained unfired, and couldn't fathom how much time remained before the explosive charge detonated and took me with it.

I stumbled to my feet and lurched toward the far tree line.

The gunfire behind me increased in volume and intensity as my attackers crested the hilltop. I approached the slope to my front in what felt like slow motion, observing bullets impacting the trees ahead of me. Puffs of smoke sprinkled against bark and leaved branches recoiled as rounds struck and tumbled past them. How had I not yet been shot? The downhill slope materialized in front of me, but was still three long paces away.

As if on cue, a single bullet struck the back plate of my body armor, and I lost all control.

I had been leaning forward into a run, and the violent impact against my spine sent me sprawling headlong with uncontrollable momentum. I flew forward and hit the ground, bounced hard on my right side, and rolled over the edge into the empty space beyond the hill.

As I soared and spun past the rock face, a deafening explosion rocked the hilltop and a blinding flash of light seared my eyes. A split second later, the shockwave passed over me; the image of the treetops whipping in the blast froze in my mind before I rolled over again to find the ground rushing toward me.

I slammed into the earth on top of my slung rifle and bounced down the hill. My vision was a blur of blue, green, and brown as sky, trees, and dirt swirled before my face. I bounced farther down the hill before hitting a tree trunk so hard that my body spun sideways as I tried to grab a bush to my left. Thorns raked my arms and face as the bush slipped from my grasp, though I was able to twist myself into a feet-first downhill slide. I looked down between my boots in search of anything to grab as I skidded on my back, but only saw clouds hovering over distant treetops.

I was twenty feet from launching over a cliff face at a speed that felt like I had been shot out of a cannon.

I dug in my heels and flung my arms to the side, clawing into the earth with gloved fingers. Trees sped past out of reach and vegetation grew sparse as the terrain dropped off into nothing. Ten feet from the edge, I saw a small tree directly in my path that was leaning perilously over the abyss. I spread my legs and placed both hands in front of my crotch, picking up speed and bracing for impact.

The trunk was perhaps three inches in width, and I slammed into it with incredible force dispersed in equal parts between my hands and groin. My sunglasses flew off, tumbling once on the ground before vanishing over the edge. The pain was a point-blank shotgun blast inside my brain, and I became so lightheaded and nauseated that I almost wished I'd gone over the side.

My body slid sideways in a 180-degree turn as I scrambled to stop it, feverishly grasping the tree trunk with both hands as my legs swung uphill. I came to rest with my back hanging over the side and my rifle dangling below me from a sling that was now wrapped around my neck at maximum tensile strength, cutting off all oxygen and blood to my brain. I was delirious with pain, and mustered all of my focus to look below me for a ledge that would allow me to simply let go of the tree and take my chances.

Instead, I saw a forty-foot drop to the talus.

My eyes registered a flash of light and a massive cloud rising from the low ground in the distance. The sound of the explosion arrived a split second later and was followed by the chatter of machine gun fire and the swooshing of faraway rockets ending in more concussions. Now moments from passing out, I released the tree with one hand to strip the M4 sling off my neck. The rifle vanished into the space below me as I returned my hand to the tree trunk.

I took a deep breath to restore what mental acuity I could before pulling myself up with all of my remaining strength. Using one hand to paw at the dirt, I hooked a leg around the tree and pulled myself into a sitting position with my legs hanging over the side. I crawled a few feet up the slope, rolled onto my back, and stared at the sky as tidal waves of pain washed over me.

The first bullet snapped into the earth a few feet to my left, blasting dirt over the cliff. I scrambled to my feet as more rounds followed from high above me on the hill. As I ran along the ledge, more bullets snapped through the trees, cracking into wood and whizzing through the air over my head. The men must have been having just as hard a time seeing me as I had when shooting at them from the hilltop.

I sprinted to a point where the hill met the cliff, then took a hard switchback and ran downhill along the descending rock face.

The gunfire stopped as I ran along the bottom of the cliff, closing the distance to my missing rifle. Fleeing straight toward my pickup site meant leading my pursuers toward Karma, who was surely standing beside the truck smoking cigarettes, unflappable amidst the gunfire and explosions resonating among the hills. The moving targets and thick vegetation rendered my pistol useless, so my only option was recovering my M4 and hoping it survived the fall.

I ran until I saw a divot of freshly turned earth and located my rifle a few meters downhill. Snatching it up, I found that it was covered in sand, a wide corner of the plastic shoulder stock had chipped off, and the suppressor was packed with dirt. Hearing a noise above me, I looked up to see one of the men standing at the top of the cliff and scanning the forest with his rifle.

He expected me to be running away, not standing directly below him. I took aim, rotated my selector lever from safe to semiautomatic, and briefly wondered whether the weapon would explode in my hands with that much dirt in the barrel. I pulled the trigger twice; the first round fired before the second malfunctioned.

As I racked the bolt to clear the failed round, the man fell over the edge, his rifle tumbling from his grasp. I threw my back against the rock face, watching his body sail past me and hit the ground with an eerie percussion accompanied by what sounded like dry branches snapping as his bones broke. Bouncing once, he rolled against a tree and stopped, motionless. His rifle crashed through a treetop and speared into the ground a short distance away from his body before pinwheeling down the mountain.

I slung my rifle and was upon him in seconds, dragging his limp body downhill and out of view from the cliff. I rolled him over, then froze when I saw his face.

A voice transmitted over the radio on his vest.

"*Remy? Remy?*"

My old friend's eyelids fluttered open. He stared into the distance before looking at me and giving me a weak half-smile.

"Hey, Slick," he drawled in his thick Alabama accent. "Thought you'd be an officer by now."

"I thought you'd still be in the Rangers." I stripped the radio off his vest and transmitted, "Your friend is fine. I'm taking his radio, and if you call for help or come down that cliff, he's dead. You can come get him in an hour, and not before."

"*Let me hear him if he's alive.*"

"This isn't a negotiation," I transmitted.

Remy said, "It's all right. I'll keep 'em back."

"Are you going to play nice?"

"You got my word."

I held the radio to his mouth and keyed it, nodding to him.

"I'm okay, guys. Just hang back, and I'll see you in an hour."

I brought the radio to my mouth. "Don't transmit again or he's dead." Stuffing the radio in my pocket, I began stripping grenades off his body and refilling the pouches on my plate carrier. His rifle magazines were meant for a different weapon, so I left them.

"That was a hell of a shot," he said.

"I learned from you, remember?"

"Hell of a fight, too. Started to think we were back in the invasion."

"You weren't so bad yourself. Do me a favor and say you never saw me before, okay?"

"I can't move anything. Give me a clean kill, Slick. I can't handle a vegetable ward."

"You'll be all right. Just let your boys come for you."

He grimaced and swallowed. "You better not leave me like this. I wouldn't do that to you."

"It might not be as bad as it looks."

"Get the fuck out of here. Let me die with some dignity."

I shook my head. "I'm sorry, brother," I said, cringing as I stood and leveled the M4 at his head. I pulled the trigger.

It clicked.

I tried to clear the malfunction again by racking the bolt, then pulled the trigger a second time.

Remington grunted and exhaled.

"Fuck, Remy, I'm sorry." I dropped the magazine and ejected the round. I partially disassembled the M4, withdrawing the bolt and blowing dirt out of it. "I don't have a suppressor on my pistol, so if I can't get this working it'll be the knife."

"I'm fine taking the knife now," he gasped.

"I still need the rifle for your friends." I blew again and began reassembling the weapon.

"You end up getting married?" he asked.

"It didn't work out."

"Well, this is just my luck. Meeting my maker as soon as Sarah's finally available."

I grinned. "You didn't want her, Remy."

"Yeah, I did."

"Ready to give this another try?"

He gave a slight nod. "Yeah, brother. See you on the other side."

"'Til next time, Remy."

I fired a single round into his face, then turned and began running down the hill.

I covered the downhill slope at a jog, eventually finding the path to my link-up site. As I approached, I saw the white pickup through the foliage. I stopped behind a tree, scanning first for the driver before turning to listen for the sounds of pursuit. Silence.

I let the rifle hang on its sling and fixed my hair as best I could with shooting gloves caked in dirt, then pulled out my earpieces and walked to the road.

Karma was standing beside the massive truck, looking at me and holding a cigarette.

Her eyes widened as I approached. "Jesus, what happened to you?"

I grabbed her waist with one hand and her cheek with the other, pinned her against the door of the truck, and kissed her.

Pulling my head back, I said, "God, you smell amazing. And I'm in an incredible amount of pain."

She put the cigarette in my lips. "You need this more than I do."

"What a lady," I said, opening the driver's side door for her.

"What a gentleman," she replied, getting behind the wheel. I let myself into the passenger seat as she started the truck and accelerated forward.

"Did you see anyone on the way in?" I asked.

"No. But it scared the shit out of me to hear gunshots instead of the mortars once the countdown was up."

"Yeah. I wasn't ecstatic about that, either. Is Matz going to kill me at the link-up?"

"Probably. You're lucky you jumped out of that plane when you did."

I took a drag, exhaling smoke through the open window. "You sure this isn't a non-smoking vehicle?"

"We're blowing up the truck in a few minutes. I won't tell Ian if you won't."

We arrived at the intersection and saw Ian's black SUV facing an adjoining road. Karma stopped the truck and reversed at an angle to block the route, leaving our ambush team's path as the only open road.

I transmitted, "Red, this is White. You want me to pop now or wait?"

"White, Red," Ian responded. "Go ahead and pop it, then consolidate. The guys are on time."

I grabbed a hiking pack from the floor behind me and unrolled the dual initiation system from the front pocket. Giving each initiator a quarter turn and a pull, I watched a puff of smoke rise from the length of time fuse. Dropping it, I started a fifteen-minute timer on my watch.

"Red, White. Burning, fifteen minutes."

"*Copy.*"

Karma locked the pickup doors and we walked to the idling SUV, then slid into the air conditioning and closed the doors behind us.

"You guys okay?" Ian turned around from the driver's seat. He saw my face and said, "Jesus, David."

"I know. I'm about to eat all the painkillers in the fucking world. Anything over the radio yet?" I adjusted the M4 between my legs and looked over my shoulder to our rear. Ian turned back around and scanned the mirrors.

"Boss transmitted they were ambush complete and moving to their getaway car. They should be there in the next minute. At the mortar site, the security force reported three dead in your explosion, and after hearing you come over their net I'm guessing you rolled up a fourth."

I hesitated. "Yeah, there was a fourth kill. Where did that patrol come from? I didn't see them until—"

Ian held up his hand to silence me as a radio in the front seat crackled to life.

"*I have visual on the element.*" There was a pause, followed by, "*I've got all three of them. No injuries. We're moving toward your position now, ETA three minutes.*"

Ian picked up the radio. "Copy. Happy hunting, guys?"

There was a short pause, and Ophie's voice came over the frequency.

"*The initial detonation flipped the lead vehicle twenty feet in the air. We were lighting up shrapnel. No survivors. It was fucking sick.*"

Boss said, "*Two minutes out from your position. Tell Suicide that—hang on a second.*" We waited without speaking until he transmitted again.

"*Midnight. Midnight. Midnight.*" Boss sounded calm, as if he were joking. Then, panicked, he screamed, "*MIDNIGHT MIDNIGHT MIDN—*"

Ian floored the gas and the wheels gained traction, the SUV fishtailing slightly on its way to full speed. Karma's wide eyes met mine, and a moment later her features vanished in an explosion of deep crimson as the first gunshots rang out.

My face was sprayed with her thick, scalding blood. I choked and gagged against the sickening stench as more bullets blasted holes through the rear windshield, sending tiny shards of glass whipping through the cab.

I wiped my eyes and blinked, seeing a blur of green through the window as our vehicle sped away. Ian was yelling something I could hear but was unable to understand. I looked at Karma, and acid rose in my throat. Her body was slumped forward unnaturally and was performing an animated jerking movement with each bump in the road. Her head was half gone, exposing a gruesome display within her shattered skull.

I picked up a fleshy, gray piece of brain matter from my lap and studied it in my fingers.

I coughed once, tried to clear my throat, and then threw up onto my rifle.

SILENCE

Nihil obstat

-Nothing stands in the way

19

September 6, 2008
Puerto Oscura, Dominican Republic

The room was white, a glowing absence of color betrayed by the approach of a single figure. Slim and lithe, she emerged from the brightness and materialized before me, perfect. Light hair grazed her shoulders, and her clear eyes locked with mine as she stepped forward, pensive, hands clasped behind the small of her back, presenting her delicate body to me. Small, hesitant steps, her frame almost shuddering with desire, stopping so close I could feel her warm exhale breathing life into me. A single hand took mine and pulled it toward her; my fingers grazed the vibrant skin below her navel for a fleeting moment as her other hand pressed a cool, dense object into my palm. She looked at me—hopeful, smiling.

I gazed down at the narrow space between us and saw a gleaming silver revolver in my hand. Her eyes rose to mine, pleading. Compliant, I placed the end of the barrel gently against my sternum. The corner of her lips curled into a curious smile as I pulled the trigger and the massive force tore through my chest, swirling life within my center before launching it backwards onto the immaculate floor. My world spun violently until the surface below me came to an abrupt stop at eye level.

I heard myself taking ragged, involuntary gasps as instinct struggled for

survival. But as a warm wetness spread outside my body so too did a cold empti-
ness grow within—

My eyes opened slowly and adjusted to the ceiling fan churning in the darkness above me. I closed them again and released a long breath, not caring to recount what had led me there that night or any other.

I lay motionless for long minutes, thoughtless and empty and seeing nothing at all.

Rolling to my side, I fumbled a cigarette from the half-empty pack on the nightstand and put it between my lips. Grabbing a lighter next to the .454 revolver, I knocked over an empty glass in the process. It rolled off the nightstand and bounced onto the carpet.

The dream had become recurring, always ending whatever sleep I managed after drinking my mind into submission. When I didn't sleep, I didn't dream.

Otherwise, Karma came to me.

The gun was always there; sometimes I put the barrel in my mouth, sometimes against my chest. Sometimes the dream ended with her standing above me, watching blankly, and sometimes I didn't get that far before waking up. But the dream always came. Sleep always ended in that glowing room.

Opening a glass door and emerging onto the third-floor balcony under a night sky, I felt a cooler than usual burst of wind accompanied by residual water pattering in droplets from the edge of the roof. Another one of the area's usual quick and tempestuous rainstorms had just rolled through, leaving a ghost of moisture in the air. Walking to the waist-high rail at the end of the balcony, I cracked the lighter to life and held the flame to the tip of my cigarette, then inhaled the first breath of smoke.

Above me, the moon presented a dull glow that brightened and dimmed as a sheet of clouds drifted slowly beneath it out to the sea. My eyes fell to the pool below me and then to the edge of the yard, which ended in a fifteen-foot wall topped with rolls of concertina wire. Tall palm trees rose blackly on the other side, their leaves rustling in the wind. From the darkness, I could hear the lonely chant of the ocean's edge as quiet waves crashed to shore and rolled back out again.

My neighborhood was a gated, walled subdivision with its own security force. Each new resident and vehicle was registered before being allowed to come and go freely. A contracted company performed landscaping and pool services after their vehicles were searched and escorted to their destination. Groceries, catered meals, uncut cocaine, top-shelf liquor, and call girls could be ordered by phone and delivered to the main gate at any time of the day or night. Even the whores were subjected to metal detector searches and had to sign in and out at the guard center. The security force conducted patrols outside the fence with dogs, continuously monitoring an extensive network of security cameras situated around the interior and exterior of the compound.

As for the community's inhabitants, there were more rumors than certainties. Mostly these rumors centered on the dollar amount of bounties that various individuals had on their lives rather than on any details about their past. I was told that a handful of such communities existed in this country alone, and many more in surrounding nations. Drug lords, snitches, hit men, and anyone with an abundance of money and enemies gather in these places. They are the elephant graveyards of crime, where retired outlaws come to ride out what time they have left.

How I got there was a story in itself. I was delivered, as promised, to the smugglers. Ian forcibly removed me from the truck with the help of another man who was waiting at our transfer point, and I stumbled forward as they half-dragged me to another vehicle. The shock was overwhelming. My head was spinning, my equilibrium gone. Covered in Karma's blood and brain matter, I was out of my mind. It was in this state that I was eventually locked into what I will call a means of transportation for the trip south. Inside, there was room and supplies for five.

I alone occupied it.

Suffice it to say that there are very complex smuggling networks established and maintained to import select commodities—including but not limited to narcotics—into the United States. The delivery vehicles for such imports are not necessarily sent back to their source empty. Any number of reliable smugglers would—and gladly do—accept a profit for the return trip. It was a long, mind-numbing process, and one that I spent in darkness and disbelief. I had not one coherent reflection from the journey south until I emerged at the destination—only scattered thoughts, flashing images of Karma's death, waves of stomach sickness and fear.

When I entered the house for the first time, I saw the dining room table arranged with five glasses and an unopened bottle of Woodford Reserve. Stepping forward, I saw a lopsided green sticker pasted on the face of the bottle. CLOSING TIME WINE & SPIRITS: $62.99.

And I began to drink.

* * *

It took days for Ian to contact me.

When he did, I strode over to the phone and snatched it by the second ring. "Who was it?"

He spoke quietly, his voice even. "You know who it was."

"What about the security force?"

"I had people monitoring their frequencies. When you took their radio, they switched to an alternate net but kept talking. They had nothing to do with the other vehicle getting hit. Or us. We beat the security forces, David. Just not the Handler."

"How could he know where we'd be?"

"He didn't have to: he knew the target. His men waited outside the security rings for us to finish the work, then hit us on our way out. The only reason you and I survived was because something tipped off Boss and he made the call. That's it."

"Where is Karma?"

"We buried her that night."

I fumbled for the chair beside me and collapsed into it. "Where?"

"In the woods."

"And the others?"

"Their bodies weren't recovered. We don't know where they are."

"How do we kill him?"

"I'm taking care of it."

"Not without me. If there's a team going in, I'm going to be part of it."

"There is. It's too late."

Tightening my grip on the phone, I leaned forward and said, "Bullshit. It will take them weeks to prepare."

"No, David, it would take months, and that's how long they've been working on it. I found something in that Sprinter van that I didn't tell Boss about."

"What the fuck does that mean?"

"It means before they died, the Five Heads had financed a team that was in the final stages of an attempt to assassinate the Handler. They agreed to negotiations to buy time until the opportunity to kill him arose."

"And you took over that team's contract after the Five Heads got killed."

"Before the sun set."

"So now it's a matter of time."

"Yes, David. That's what I'm trying to tell you."

"Okay." I sighed, looking over at the .454 maintaining its lonely vigil on the nightstand. "Ian, I need to know when it's done."

* * *

Taking a final drag off the cigarette, I bitterly tossed it off the balcony to join its fallen comrades on the lawn, then returned to the house. I walked to the nightstand and retrieved the revolver, then made my way to the master bathroom and turned on the light.

I stared at the face in the mirror.

Devoid of purpose, drinking and waiting for the phone to ring, I had begun writing again. Putting the story of the team to words became my sole purpose, my only reason for living.

The writing took over my life. I would sit at the computer all day as pages poured out of me, then look up and realize I hadn't consumed anything in eight or nine hours besides vast quantities of caffeine, nicotine, and alcohol. I had never written anything other than scattered introspection and late-night ramblings, and suddenly I found myself buried a hundred pages deep in a single manuscript.

Since I couldn't tell the team's story without detailing the path that led me to them, I had to dredge up past memories. I revisited old writings, wading through written memories of war, of Afghanistan and Iraq and a failed engagement, of darkness and drinking and jumping, of acting out the self-destructive fantasies of a living death wish in the twilight hours while the world slept.

I read long-forgotten thoughts and composed new ones so ghastly in written form that the collection represented little more than a slow, spiraling descent into insanity. Once the writing was done, I stood, eviscerated, looking at a twelve-foot tapeworm that I almost wished had never been discovered.

And then, just like that, it was over.

When I began, I typed the story carefully, as if the transcript would vanish before it was completed. Eventually, I progressed to crashing through the pages, until one day I was suddenly rereading the work as if it belonged to someone else, as if I didn't have the power to change it. The story no longer belonged to me. It was a cryptic tablet dug out of the earth, isolated, incomprehensible, repulsive— something to be left alone or passed to an outside party for analysis. I chose to leave it alone, and lay in bed that night with a feeling of closure, but not achievement.

Since then, I had written nothing.

I looked at the reflection of my face in the mirror. Lifting the revolver, I put the barrel in my mouth. My fingertip made sensual contact with the smooth, curved metal of the trigger. Just a slight touch, just a caress. Rounding second base in suicide contemplation.

Eight pounds of pressure. My mind retrieved that particular piece of data unsolicited, its only conscious thought.

Withdrawing the barrel, I opened the cylinder and dumped the six massive bullets into my palm, setting them one at a time onto the sink.

I looked in the mirror for a long time—at the deep green, unflinching eyes; at my dark blond hair that was casually askew; at the stubble on my chin and cheeks that appeared premeditated rather than a product of my unwillingness to shave. Friends had told me I looked like a movie star or a model. I thought I looked sinister, that my eyes only appeared bright because of the dark circles that highlighted them.

The stoic face stared back at me, unwilling to reveal its secrets. My mind's singular thought: *you'll see. Keep writing, and you'll see. I will tell you nothing; you will find out for yourself.*

I checked the cylinder to make sure all the chambers were empty, closed it, and put the gun back in my mouth.

Made eye contact with the man in the mirror.

Pulled the trigger.

Click.

An instant pang of adrenaline—the forbidden kind, the kind that arises when you illegally BASE jump from a high-rise apartment building in the middle of the night in a New York City borough where getting arrested meant a double felony. Good, clean fun, unless you get caught.

You're not supposed to be doing this.

Guilty adrenaline, the forbidden kind.

I removed the gun and rechecked the cylinder, then selected a single round from the sink. Sliding it into a chamber, I spun the cylinder and closed it. I returned the barrel to my mouth.

I looked into the dancing green eyes in the mirror.

Click.

The adrenaline rush returned, stronger this time. I put my finger over the trigger again.

The phone began to ring. I pulled the trigger.

Click.

I walked back into the master bedroom and answered the phone with my free hand.

"Is he dead?"

"The attempt was today. They failed."

"What do you mean, 'they failed?'"

"None of them made it out."

"So he's still alive? I've got a solution for that, Ian, and it's what I told you in the first place."

"It's not that simple, David."

"Yes, it is. You're the one with all the theories on this guy. Teach me what you know, and I'll take care of him. Boss said the Handler could be killed, so I know it can be done."

"Boss didn't see what I saw today. It's just you and me now, and the Handler has gone into hiding. That limits our options to one path, and I'm not sure either of us wants to take it."

"I'm seeing Karma every night, Ian. Don't tell me I don't want to take it. If there's only one way, tell me what it is."

"That's a conversation we need to have in person."

"Then let's meet."

He hesitated. "Let me set up the transport and call you back with the details."

I hung up the phone and stood in the darkness, alone with the thoughts in my head and the ringing in my ears.

My eyes drifted to the .454, my only constant companion amidst the solitude. I opened the cylinder to see what the next trigger squeeze would have yielded, then closed it and looked toward the balcony. The longer I spent in that house, the more certain I became that my last moment, wherever and whenever it occurred, would be with that weapon in my hand.

Finis Coronat Opus.

The ending crowns the work.

Offer of Revenge:
American Mercenary #2

An avenging survivor. An unconquerable enemy. And one impossible betrayal...

David Rivers wants vengeance.

But there's only one way to kill his greatest enemy—David must first join the secretive organization that slaughtered the only family he had.

To prove his allegiance, he enters a life-or-death battle in the badlands of Somalia.

But the closer David gets to his target, the more he realizes that the betrayal of his team was not as random as he thought.

Someone inside the organization seems to know his true purpose, and that could mean only one thing:

David might not have been the sole survivor after all.

Get your copy today at
severnriverbooks.com/series/the-american-mercenary

ACKNOWLEDGMENTS

A team of six people deserves credit for the completion of this work.

My first thanks belongs to my sister, Julie. In title, she filled the role of content editor. In reality, she was the first person to read each revision and has, by now, far exceeded the word count of the finished novel in the amount of written feedback she has provided. Her keen observations and ruthless input have pushed the story further than I thought it could go, and she singlehandedly and mercilessly prevented countless abysmal drafts from seeing the light of day as I bungled my way through the process of writing my first novel.

There are few people I can count as a mentor, and fewer still who also qualify as a friend. Derek is both. He served as my first beta reader when this work was in its infancy, and he was the first person to tell me I should pursue writing beyond a part-time hobby. His challenge and inspiration has guided me toward the dark road I now find myself on, for better or worse. I couldn't be more grateful.

The great Ernie Young next deserves my thanks. A lifelong friend, college roommate, astute beta reader, and an Aston Martin owner, he has been one of my most faithful and steadfast confidantes. His opinions on every facet of my work have been beyond influential, and I have every confidence and hope that they will continue to guide me throughout the series.

Master Sergeant John "JB" Presley has been a larger-than-life figure whose feedback as a beta reader—particularly one whose time in combat alone encompasses nearly a third of his life—was instrumental in crafting this story. Novel aside, it was an honor to serve alongside him on his fifteenth and sixteenth deployments.

No budding manuscript is complete until a professional editor turns it into a bloodbath, and Cara Quinlan executed that vital task for this book. Her skillful application of expertise guided me in elevating this story to its full potential, and her patient guidance and never-ending answers along the way have ensured that the sequel will enjoy a much better starting point than its predecessor.

Most importantly, thank you to my beautiful and long-suffering wife, Amy. Her eternal loyalty and support withstood countless late nights and early mornings as I toiled over this work between deployments, after which she tirelessly served as a remarkably keen beta reader. In spite of all this, her demand that I spend the first six months after leaving the military unreservedly following my passion has ensured that I will enjoy at least half a year as a full-time author. There is no greater gift she could bestow.

ABOUT THE AUTHOR

Jason Kasper is the USA Today bestselling author of the Spider Heist, American Mercenary, and Shadow Strike thriller series. Before his writing career he served in the US Army, beginning as a Ranger private and ending as a Green Beret captain. Jason is a West Point graduate and a veteran of the Afghanistan and Iraq wars, and was an avid ultramarathon runner, skydiver, and BASE jumper, all of which inspire his fiction.

Sign up for Jason Kasper's reader list at
severnriverbooks.com/authors/jason-kasper

jasonkasper@severnriverbooks.com

Printed in the United States
by Baker & Taylor Publisher Services